Random Thoughts of a Strange Mind

by
Kenneth Lee McGee

For Everyone
Who Appreciates
A Good Yarn

These stories have been written
over the course of several years
though often quickly.

Some were written for my own amusement.
Others were written for family and friends.

Many of these adventures are adapted
from the blogs on my website.

All are meant to be lighthearted entertainment.

Since my editor was busy making dinner,
I didn't bother to edit these stories.
The mistakes that existed on the website
are still here, so deal with it.
Okay, dinner is almost ready and my editor
insisted I do some editing or else she
won't iron my underwear.
I did just enough to trick her.

Table of Contents

101 Ways To Prepare Eggplant

Kohlrabi: The Unappreciated Veggie

The Critic

Summertime In Sunny Severnaya

Casablanca

Don't Worry, Dear, It Was Only a Small Fire

Not That Choir... *The Choir!*

An Entomologist's Work Is Just Bee-ginning

Behold The Terrors Within

Why Can't Car Keys and Electrical Outlets Be Friends?

Notre Dame Defeats the Electoral College... Again

Mom! The TV Repairman Is Here!

Santa Claus Is Real... I Met Him In Person

A Walk Into Town

The Junior Class Carnival (and Other
        Important High School Activities)

The Farm

Yesterday I Sat On a Bee and It Didn't Sting Me

Random Thoughts of a Strange Mind

Have you ever wondered who was the first person to eat an eggplant? Or a rutabaga? Why did they think this might be something tasty to have for dinner? And why does adding bacon to something always make it taste better? With the possible exception of orange Jello.

How can you tell which end of a hot dog to eat first? If you start at the wrong end, can you turn it around and meet in the middle?

Harpo Marx proved you can burn a candle at both ends.

Has a turtle ever actually beaten a rabbit in a race? If they did race, what were the Vegas odds?

Why are there so many Bible names like Methusaleah, Zerubabel, Jehoshaphat, Zurishaddai, Nebuchadnezzar, Malachi, Kerenhappuch, Ehud and Uzzah? But then there are also David, John, Peter, James, Phoebe, Priscilla, Jason and Mary.

Who was the first pregnant woman to ask for a dill pickle and ice cream in the middle of the night? Was it Eve?

Why did Noah let mosquitos onto his boat?

Before Julius Caesar decided to add two months to the calendar, were the years shorter? Is that why people in the Old Testament lived so much longer?

Why do we drive on a parkway, and park in a driveway? (I didn't title this blog 'Original Thoughts of a Strange Mind')

Who came up with the term palindrome? Or the word neologism?

Who was the optimist who thought deer could read those signs along the Interstate and obey them? You know which ones I mean.

If mustard seeds are so small, how did we find them in the first place?

If water is wet, how can there be dry ice?

Do other languages beside English have so many contronyms? Or homophones? I know of no other, but yet here in the states we hear examples every day too many times to count. It's enough to make me slam on my brake and break down and cry. Let me throw out this often overlooked model to wind up this puzzle.

Is there another word for synonym?

How was glass invented? Did someone pile sand up in a window and then burn it?

Can something ever be in whack?

Why do drive through ATMs have Braille on the instructions?

If you take a large byte out of an Apple, can you see the core?

How does a schoolbus driver close the door when he leaves?

Who places those 'Do not walk on the grass' signs in the middle of the yard?

Who decided sliced bread was the best thing ever? And what was it before the bread slicer was invented?

How do you tune bagpipes? If you figure it out, who's going to be brave enough to tell the Scotsman wearing a kilt how to do it?

Why is the alphabet in the order it is? Was it decided by a committee?

Along that same line. Why is there an extra R in February? Who decided on the spelling of Wednesday? Who decided it would be funny to put silent letters at the mbeginning of so kmany pwords?

Who invented string cheese and why isn't it longer?

While we're on the subject of dairy products, who first tried to milk a cow, and why did the cow let him?

If you drive a white Corvette and break the speed limit in the Antarctic, can the police see your car?

Who decided on the shape of Maryland? Were they drunk or just teasing West Virginia?

If ice was totally transparent, would you be afraid to walk to the North Pole?

Did Emo Rubik ever invent anything else? Is he a one-cube wonder?

If Carl Wilhelm Scheele discovered Oxygen in 1772, what did people breath before that?

Did Walt Disney build a better mousetrap? (This one might take a while to understand)

What kind of computer would Albert Einstein use? What kind would Isaac Newton use?

13

Why would you ever visit a psychic? If they were really psychic, they would have won the lottery and moved to Sun Valley, Idaho.

If no trees grow above the treeline, why does hair grow above your hairline?

If someone whacks you with a baseball bat made from a hardwood tree, does it hurt more than a bat made from a softwood tree?"

Would teepees have round tops if Eskimos had lived in Arizona or Nebraska?

Why doesn't the DMV hire better photographers?

Why is the price of cars manufactured in China dependent on one single butterfly in Argentina?

If James Dean had left the house a minute later, would there be a *Rebel Without a Cause, Part 5*?

If you can't see the forest for the trees, why can you see a sand dune?

If God doesn't have a sense of humor, why would He (or She) put a fish's eyes on opposite sides of its head?

The last one. If con is the opposite of pro, is Congress the opposite of progress?

The Apolitical Blues, Part I

The other day my wife referred to me as the most apolitical person she knows. I thought about it, and told her she needs to get out more. But it's probably true. If someone mentions 'Presidential Debate' to me, I think of Kennedy and Nixon. Nixon was the winner in my opinion, but he didn't look good on camera. But he sure knew how to erase a tape!

It's not that I'm completely apathetic, but I can't get into the mudslinging. And I'm not talking about the candidates. I am referring to the ordinary man, or woman, on the street who feels a need to disparage any candidate who doesn't believe the way they do.

A wise man once told me to never get into a discussion about politics or religion because there is no way to win an argument on those subjects. Since Mr. Lincoln was pretty smart (except about his choices of plays) I try to follow his advice.

My wife on the other hand knows everything about politics. She can tell you who voted for or against House Bill #458-K-6238MN and the exact wording of the thing the leader of the majority party snuck in there to benefit the people in his district. I don't remember who ran for president against James Polk.

Ooops! My wife just informed me there have been other presidents after Polk.

My favorite president has always been Millard Fillmore. Why? Because you can trust a man with the name Millard. Imagine the battles he fought as a kid trying to keep some bully named Joe from beating him up for no other reason than he didn't like the name Millard. To kinda quote J.R. Cash... If I have another son, I'm gonna name him Millard... or Bill or George... anything but Sue.

I learned in school that if just one more person in each local precinct had voted for Nixon instead of Kennedy, then Watergate would have never happened. One person's vote can make a difference, and in Chicago it doesn't matter if that person is... well, I won't go there.

I always liked the slogan "Vote early and vote often." One person can make a difference if they vote enough times.

I always enjoyed listening to Ronald Reagan. Not only was he born in Illinois, but he was a sports commentator in his early days. I especially enjoyed him in the movie *Santa Fe Trail*, which also starred Alan Hale, who is the father of Jonas Grumby. Better known as the Skipper in Gilligan's Island. I mean the actor who played... never mind. that's a different blog. Anyone who could upstage a talking mule has my vote.

I've heard it said that money wins elections. Case in point would be the aforementioned Kennedy vs. Nixon, or better yet, the campaign between William Henry Harrison and Martin Van Buren. Both candidates spent over $614 on their campaign and Harrison won because he used coins instead of paper money. Van Buren later became knows for his invention of solar-powered windshield washers (the idea didn't catch on at the time because automobiles weren't invented and horses balked at the idea of warsher* blades going back and forth across their eyes) *Where I come from the word is pronounced with an R inserted. So much depends on proper timing.

I support our politicians... have you seen how high the gas tax is?... I think they are doing their best. At what I don't know, but to quote one of my favorite authors... 'An effort was made.'

To quote Lowell George... I have a apolitical blues and it's the meanest blues of all. I don't care if you're John Wayne I just don't want to take no calls. No calls. If it was good enough for Van Halen, it's good enough for me.

P.S. My name is George Washington, and I approved this blog.

The St. Louis Cardinals Should Change Their Name, Part 1

Now before you get all excited and up in arms, let me provide this disclaimer. I have been a St. Louis Cardinal fan since I first heard Harry Caray on the radio in Grandma's kitchen late on a Friday night in the summer of 1942. For those of you too young to remember, Harry Caray was a Cardinal broadcaster long before he was demoted to the minor leagues and served out his time broadcasting for both fans of the Chicago Subs.

I was a Cardinal fan before I knew there were other major league teams. I wasn't smart enough to realize they had to have an opponent. My cousin Paul clued me in to that reality on the bus going home after school in first grade. Hey! I was only seventeen at the time, and had spent most of those early years in a cave hiding from Indians... I mean Native Americans.

I have a pennant on the wall in my office from 1962. It's hanging up right behind me. I'll turn the computer around so you can see it... See? It's really there. It has been in my possession since I was knee-high to a short-legged grasshopper. I also have a pennant my dad brought home from the University of Cincinnati when they won the NCAA tournament back in '61 and '62. I like to keep things around for a long time. Just ask my wife. We've been married over 128 years and never had an argument. Yes, honey, I put it in the blog about how smart you are.

I credit our long, successful marriage to a selective hearing loss. But I digress.(I love digressing in blogs. Since no one reads them, I can write whatever foolishness I want.) The reason I think the Cardinals should change their name is not because of some perceived racial slur, but because a close friend of mine is a birdwatcher. He's not an ornithologist. There is a difference. He is an amateur nature guy who likes to watch birds. He's from England, so I can understand his behavior. (Please! Someone get that joke. I made a bet with my wife and can't afford to lose the 50 Cent. (Yo! My man Curtis James Jackson.)

Another reason I feel the Cardinals should change their name is because... well... they have won so many pennants and World Series. I feel they should give other teams a chance to win. I mean teams like the Subs or the Pirates (can I still call them the Pirates, or did they need to change their name to 'Disreputable Sailors With Beards Who Go Around Saying Arrgh and Matey' all the time?) Those teams have loyal fans, or at least one fan, who deserve to see their team be successful more than once a century. Like that will happen for the Subs. I like to root for the underdog at times. Though I suffer immensely at every Notre Dame football loss. It wouldn't bother me if they won every game by 50 points. Yeah, I am a fan of the UConn Lady Huskies, too. They won like a thousand games in a row. (To be accurate, it was 111.) Personally, I would love to see the Detroit Lions play the Cleveland Browns in the Super Bowl. Unless it means more commercials starring Baker Mayberry and his house. You never see a commercial starring Mitch Trubisky. Right? Remember him. He used to play for the Bears.

Who roots for the Patriots? Not me. Though I respect them for their consistency. (Who wouldn't win the division against the Jets, Bills and Dolphins?) And their ability to cheat without getting caught too often. Am I bitter about the interception on the goal line? (Seattle Seahawk reference for those non-football fans.) You better believe it. Or the mental error that cost the Kansas City Chiefs (The Native American Leaders, I mean.) a chance to be in the Super Bowl against the New Orleans Saints (Ooops! My bad. The Saints were robbed and the Rams [I can't keep track of what city they play in now. They've moved around more often than the renter who refuses to pay his landlord.] were in the Super Bowl). Take a name like The Saints. Can anyone argue about that name? Even the Pope is a fan of Saints. I'm glad Tom Brady Bunch is now playing for the Buccaneers. (I mean the 'Disreputable Sailors With Beards Who Go Around Saying Arrgh and Matey, Part 2') If he is the Greatest Of All Time (GOAT for short) then let him win a Super Bowl with Tampa Bay. They are the equivalent of the St. Louis Browns. (Perennial losers who had to move to Baltimore.) If he can win with that team at the age of 73, then I will give him credit as the GOAT. Right now I think Bobby Douglas was the GOAT. What other quarterback can throw a football from Wrigley Field to Soldier Field and hit his target with absolute, consistent accuracy .003% of the time. He could throw the ball not over buildings, but through them! Let me tell you Grasshopper, that is a gun for an arm.

But the real reason I think the Cardinals should change their name is... so I can write a blog about why they should always be called the ST. LOUIS CARDINALS.

The Master Builder

1 CORINTHIANS 3:10 (KING JAMES VERSION)

"According to the grace of God which is given unto me, as a wise masterbuilder, I have laid the foundation, and another buildeth thereon. But let every man take heed how he buildeth thereupon."

God gives us many different gifts. I used Google to find a list. Among the most common are Wisdom, Knowledge, Faith, Gifts of Healing, Working of Miracles and others. I believe we are all gifted though many of us fail to use or even realize our gifts. It makes sense that God gives us a variety of talents. Imagine, if we were all given the gift of playing the drums, who would play the melody on the piano. Anyone can play the drums. I've been doing it for years, and recently learned how to distinguish the left stick from the right. Now I'm a master drummer.

This blog is to draw attention to, and thank, a friend from church. In order not to embarrass him, I will use a fictitious name. I will call him... Bill Griffin. That's common enough to protect his privacy. Anyway, this person, whose real name is something totally different, has been blessed with many gifts or talents. He is a gifted vocalist. He has been a faithful follower of Christ for fifty years, give or take. I first met Bill, or George or whatever name I was using, almost sixty years ago. He is a humble man and more importantly he occasionally laughs at my lame jokes.

This fictitious person I'm calling Bill is also a master builder. A master carpenter, a brilliant electrician, a capable plumber. Before you ask for his number to hire him, he's retired and has four and a half grandchildren to spoil. Our church is indeed fortunate to have... Bill... as a member. He has fixed everything that's ever broken in the church. He's made usable closets out of wasted space. Did I mention he can paint better than Mickey Angelo and Lenny da Vinci put together? His latest project is nearing completion and is spectacular. I can't give away the details because it is top secret (because of the COVID-19 situation) until the church reopens for indoor services. However, I can reveal it is truly an astounding reformation.

I cannot replace a broken lightbulb without reading the manual for several days. If my car needs an oil change, I trade it in. I remember how to fill the gas tank, I think. It's been two months since I had to add gas so I should read the owner's manual again. There are many people who learn the skills needed to do what... Bob... or was it... Ben... No it was Bill, accomplish, but I've never met one with his humble attitude and Christian character.

Hopefully, I've written enough about my friend to thoroughly embarrass him if he ever reads this, or more likely, someone tells him about it. I want to recognize him for all the work he has done and continues to do for the church and his family and friends.

Thank you, Bill and Happy Birthday (It's not until December but I thought I'd get an extra like if I add it here.)

If You Never Played Wiffle Ball As a Kid...

If you never played wiffle ball as a kid, you don't know what you missed. Nowadays, people play wiffle ball like a real sport. They play on regular baseball fields, have real tournaments and crown champions. I even watched a tournament on TV.

But that's not the kind of wiffle ball I'm talking about. My cousin Paul and I played REAL wiffle ball. One man (boy) against another. You had to chase down every ball that was hit or swung at and missed. Foul balls hit over the fence were usually the batter's responsibility to retrieve. And we liked to play in areas with fences. If at all possible, we didn't use the wiffle balls with holes in them. We would but the solid ones. They were harder to throw curves, but more realistic. They even had seams in the plastic to imitate real baseballs. Plus, they lasted longer.

We would pick a team. I was always the Cardinals. He was usually the Yankees. We would create a lineup. We might have invented Fantasy Baseball without realizing it. Anyway, you made your lineup and you had to bat the way your player did. That's how we learned to hit from both sides of the plate. We would even imitate the player's stance. Try hitting out of Stan Musial's stance. It ain't easy.

Part of the fun of wiffle ball is finding, or creating, the place to play. One of my all-time favorite places was my grandparents' garden. They lived on a farm in the country outside of Kinmundy, Illinois. When they were able, they had a garden directly behind the house. The garden was fenced on all four sides and was almost a perfect square. I can see the wheels turning in your head. A perfect square. Fences. Grass. A nearby house. All of these contributed to the perfect diamond on which to play wiffle ball. The garden wasn't large enough to play real baseball. The proximity of the house made that impossible. However, wiffle balls don't normally travel as far or break windows. Later in their life, they were unable, or didn't need, a garden for their sustenance. That's when Paul and I created our own Fields of Dreams.

Since we were playing one on one, much like we did in basketball, we created our own set of rules. Catching the ball in the air was obviously an out, but there were other ways to retire a better. Catching a grounder before it reached a certain line was an out. There were rules for doubles, triples and homeruns. We had a fence, so a homerun was obvious. If you hit the ball over the fence it was a homerun. Simple, right? We even had a shorter right field than left field, but if the wind was blowing from the east, it was nearly impossible to hit the ball out of the park in right. In straight center field was the 'turkey house' as we had always called the building. There were never any turkeys kept in there in our childhood, but maybe at one time. Anyway, it was something to aim for. In right field, maybe six feet inside the fence was the Concord grape arbor. I loved sucking the juice out of the grapes and spitting out the pulp and seeds. Approximately twenty feet past the left-center field fence was the house. It would take a prodigious wallop to hit the house, but I accomplished it one at least one occasion. Paul may not remember it, but I do. Unfortunately, we didn't have statisticians recording every pitch like real baseball or any form of instant replay. There will never be a YouTube video of our games. We used the garden as our field for many years, but eventually, we grew up.

After college, Paul moved to an A frame house in the country north of Bloomington/Normal. His backyard became our Fenway Park. We had our own Green Monster except it wasn't green and was in right field. It was the back of the house and garage. It was close enough to land a homerun on the roof with a pop-up if the wind was from the north. However, if the wind was from the south (blowing right over the house) it was nearly impossible to smack one out of the park. Case in point. I was batting lefty and nailed a pitch. I couldn't have connected more solidly in a hundred years. The ball flew halfway to the moon and was hit hard enough to go completely over the house except for the wind. I hit it too good and too high. Paul patiently waited for the ball to return. By the time it came back to earth, the wind had carried it into play and Paul caught it for an out. Sometimes it's better to be lucky than good.

It might have been at the A frame where we first used a strike zone. The strike zone would be a rectangular box placed behind the hitter. To be called a strike, a pitch need only hit the box. It didn't matter from which direction. You could theoretically curve a ball from behind the batter, hit the edge of the box and be a strike. Probably never happened, but possible. In our rules one strike was an out.

Now I am too old to play baseball, or even checkers, but I bet Paul and I could still find a Garden of Dreams somewhere and manage to play our version of the World Series. I would bribe one of the grandkids into retrieving the ball though.

The Typewriter Virus, Part 1

In early December of 2019 I published *New Priorities – Emmy's Story, Part 16* and prepared to write the next book in the series. The outline was finished and I knew where I wanted to take the story. But for some reason I wasn't ready to begin working. I took time off for the holidays and figured I would start in January after my birthday. January flew by and then so did February without a single word written.

I decided to take more time off and travel the world. I've spent time overlanding across the lower states, spent several weeks exploring Alaska and then headed back to the Southwest. I love the desert and plateaus of Utah and Arizona. I even ventured into California and up the Pacific coast.

Lately, I've been visiting Europe – I love old castles, British palaces, French chateaus and Italian villages clinging to the cliffs of the Amalfi Coast. I've enjoyed walks across my ancestral home of England and Scotland. I've lost myself in County Kerry of Ireland. I know more about Dublin than Bono and The Edge put together. It is so easy to get around London using the "Tube." I still can't fathom how builders managed nearly a thousand years ago to create Gothic Cathedrals that soar into the clouds.

I've explored the world without leaving my office. Isn't YouTube a magical world!

But now it's time to get back to work, and I realize why I waited four months to continue with the journey of Emmy, Kenny and all the other characters in South Hampshire. It was because my old-fashioned typewriter had contracted a virus. I'm not making light of the world situation. It's much too serious and it would have been a mistake to write the next Emmy book without including it. The Emmy series has been written in the past, but now the timeline has caught up to 2020. Though we are unsure about how long our lives will be affected, I still firmly believe God has everything under control. I even went to church this morning without leaving my home. Now it's time to see how my little world of characters responds to my typewriter virus.

The TV Westerns of My Youth, Part 1

Lately, I have been watching old Westerns using the Amazon Prime Video channel. As a kid I loved *The Lone Ranger*, *The Cisco Kid* and to a lesser extent Roy Rogers and Gene Autry. In case you're wondering about the cover photo, Scout is on the left, then Tonto, The Lone Ranger and Silver on the right. The horses were often better actors than the humans, but I doubt they were paid as much. Thinking of the singing cowboy stars, who ever really thought cowboys played guitars and sang campfire songs on those cattle drives? They did get to eat cool food. Beans, biscuits and bacon. The three Bs of a healthy diet. I can just smell the... never mind.

Hopalong Cassidy was one of the first Westerns to make the switch to the small screen. Television. I don't remember watching William Boyd, the actor who played Hopalong, as often as the other heroes of the Old West, but after watching it on Amazon, I enjoyed it as much, and though it pains me to say it, even more than The Lone Ranger and The Cisco Kid. Though I still love hearing the 1812 Overture and the intro music used for *The Cisco Kid*. Sacrilege you say! The Lone Ranger stood for law and justice and everything a young boy should aspire to become. (Other than the mask which modern facial recognition software would render obsolete.)

As near as I can tell, there are three essential parts to any good Western (I'm talking about Westerns for kids, not the adult stuff like *Bonanza, Gunsmoke, Wagon Train, Rawhide* and *Mister Ed.*)

First there must be a long chase scene. The horses were awesome creatures. They could chase at full speed for miles through terrain that would completely disable a custom Jeep Wrangler Rubicon. On a side note, why are modern horse races like the Kentucky Derby, Belmont Stakes and others so short? Two minutes and they're over. Silver, Scout, Diablo, Loco, Trigger and Champion could race like the wind for half the show. Another version of the chase scene would be the runaway stagecoach or wagon. Usually with a helpless female on board, or else the driver would be miraculously shot with one of the hundreds of bullets fired in his general direction. Again, the team of horses had more stamina and endurance than a diesel locomotive.

The second part essential to any good Western serial was the shootout. And I mean shoot until your hand must have cramped up! Have you ever tried to count how many shots are fired in a typical shootout? I have, but I lost track at 2,148 shots fired without reloading. And even more amazing is the fact that only a small percentage of those thousands of bullets ever reached their intended human target. A blind geriatric from a nursing home (before COVID-19) would have a higher success rate. Yet most often the times when those bullets did hit a human, it was the hand holding the gun. Cowboys, sheriffs and gunslingers could be firing at close range at each other for the obligatory five minute shoot out scene without hitting anything. But then would come the miracle shot (often from a greater distance than the range of modern cruise missiles) knocking the gun from the bad guys' hand. And no the bad guys did not always wear black cowboy hats. Hopalong Cassidy often, usually, wore a black hat and black outfit. (Must be where Johnny Cash got the inspiration for his song.)

The third part would be the female character. Though the names were changed, the character didn't. The female lead was most often: coming out West after going to school back East; the younger sister of the sheriff or other good guy; sometimes a widow with kids; (Okay, there was some variety in the female characters, but hot much and ignore my punctuation. I used semi-colons because it's easier than holding down the shift key.) The lead cowboy was usually a gentleman, though the Cisco Kid liked to flirt with every lady in the episode. (Though production budgets normally restricted the number of female characters to one per episode.) At least Roy Rogers was married to Dale Evans, but why wasn't her character called Dale Rogers?

The fourth part (Ooops! Lost count) was the climax. It was usually a combination of a shoot out on horses (Again lasting several minutes at speeds Mustangs struggle to maintain) or in a cabin somewhere in the middle of nowhere. (The cabin looked the

27

same in every episode and on every different series – again with the exception of the Ponderosa on *Bonanza*.) I'm amazed at how much glass the producers had to replace every episode. Bullets apparently were stopped by walls thin enough to poke a hole in with a McDonald's straw. (paper not plastic) I suppose whoever owned the cabins had insurance that covered window breakage. In the end, the bad guys who be caught and sent to jail. The old prospector would regain his stolen mine (which often produced more gold and silver than the entire Klondike and Colorado gold rushes combined. The rustled cattle would be returned to their rightful owner in time to be butchered. The stolen gold and paper money would be returned to the bank vaults which looked as secure as the bathroom door in my house and all would be right in the West. (Until the next episode which would start with a chase scene, shoot out and...

Random Thoughts of a Strange Mind, Part 2

I found this little article in my folder of Website blogs, and though it's short and maybe incomplete, I decided to post it to fulfill my PR company's desire for new material.

Have you ever wondered what life would be like if all of today's modern technology existed with the exception of maps? Imagine self-driving cars without any guidance.

Imagine everyone on TV speaking in Shakespearean English.

What if checkers was the most complicated board game and chess was played by infants.

Babe Ruth's first season with the Yankees was 100 years ago. There are people still alive who might have gone to those games. I bet they could afford a hot dog and a Coke back then.

Zoom used to be the marketing strategy for an automobile company. (Zoom Zoom)

Only outlaws in the Old West wore masks. (and The Lone Ranger)

Books had to be held in your hands and opened page by page to read them. (Please buy one of my books! I need the dollar I earn in royalties to pay for all the masks I have to buy.)

School was actually a building you took a bus to get to. Unless you had to walk like I did. Ten miles uphill each way... you know the rest.

I wish a corona was still a typewriter. (That's from a song, but I can't think of the title right now. Help me out.)

Why are my grandkids able to write their own computer programs, and I struggle to turn on my flip phone?

What ever happened to all those kiosks that used to be in every parking lot. You could pull up in your car, hand them your film (do any cameras still use film?) come back the next day and they would give you actual printed photographs. Just a thought. Where did the person working in those kiosks go to the bathroom? There was barely enough room for them to turn around.

I miss the lady who used to sit in the little glass box that stuck out from the top floor of the Sears store in downtown SoHam (excuse me downtown Joliet) She would announce where you could find an empty parking space.

Is the Dollar Store an off shoot of the White Store that used to be downtown? Not everything in the Dollar Store costs a dollar, and not everything in The White Store was white.

I dislike canned crowd noise nearly as much as the canned laughter from old TV sitcoms. (If you aren't a football fan, you may ignore this comment.)

I think Joe Walsh should run for president because *You Can't Argue With a Sick Mind.*

The World's Best Taco Salad

I hate to brag , but I will. My taco salad is the best in the world!

That's a rather bold claim, I know, but I'm only exaggerating a little. I have several friends who will back up my claim (and I didn't pay them to say it well, not too much.). I have been making taco salad using this top secret recipe for close to fifty years. In fact, I might have been the first person to make taco salad. I have no scientific data to back this up, but I could probably create some.

I believe the reason for my success as a preeminent taco salad maker stems from my attention to detail. I've heard it said God is in the details, or was that the devil? Regardless, I make my taco salad to exacting details. Never let it be said my taco salad is ordinary. One of the secrets to doing any job professionally is to use the right tools for the right job. I take pride in having used the same professional tools for the last half-century. If you buy the best tools and take care of them they will last a lifetime. I have the proof.

I am going to reveal my steps for preparing the world's best taco salad. First, you must prepare the space to make it. I suggest building a kitchen no smaller than 4,162 square feet (a perfect square is preferred but not completely essential) I also suggest a wooden kitchen island. I have discovered that growing my own trees works best. You need to purchase a minimum of 67.4 acres of woodlands to grow your trees. Many people scoff at the idea, however, it has been proven year after year that the Sigillaria tree makes the best butcher blocks. Unfortunately, this tree has been extinct for thousands of years, so it is rather difficult to find. I buy mine at Noah's Rare Woods in downtown Ur-By-The-Sea. The shop is located next door to Beans 'n' More. Ask for Noah and mention my name and he will give you a 3.135593446 percent discount. (You must show him my photo to receive full discount)

Now to the basic steps. Once you have purchased all necessary ingredients (Due to government secrecy laws pertaining to national defense, I cannot divulge the complete list of ingredients) it is time to make your taco salad. If you do not have the vital large yellow Tupperware bowl, you can use a yellow metal bucket provided it contains the correct amount of rust. You should assemble the following items in a straight row on your Sigillaria tree butcher block making sure to keep 3.71 inches between each can. Line them up in this order kidney beans (light or dark, I prefer the dark ones but I have extremely sensitive taste buds. Many people will not be able to distinguish between them)), diced green chilies, xxxx xxxxxx (see above note about secrecy laws) black olives, 1 quart of Kearney's 50 weight motor oil (this doesn't go in the taco salad but I like how the can looks next to the olives) Let the sun shine on these cans for 11 minutes and 18 seconds (except in February when you need to add 28 seconds) take your Decker & Blackmoore titanium can opener from the safe and use it to open the cans IN THE SAME ORDER AS THEY ARE LINED UP! This is essential! Never let the cans get closer than 3.54 inches to one another. Drain the kidney beans (African American beans can be substituted for variety) use your 11.36 inch number 24863 orange plastic strainer and rinse them for 68.43 seconds under ordinary tap water. Room temperature water is fine. I mean who really cares. Add the beans to the center of your large yellow Tupperware bowl taking care not to stack more than two beans on top of each other. Open the chilies (I use Russell Lamborighianas chilies exclusively because the company pays me millions of dollars for the use of my photo on the cans) and carefully and slowly, allowing the chilies to breath, layer them on top of the beans. Next add the black olives. It doesn't matter what brand because who in the world believes there are enough virgin olives in the world to make all that oil (let alone extra virgins) add the olives. DO NOT MIX THE INGREDIENTS TOGETHER AT THIS POINT! You may be very tempted to use your Brady-Welker stainless steel spoon at this time but be patient. The mixing comes later. At this point, and only at the point, you can open the Kearney's 50 weight motor oil and fill your lawn mower. Once this is finished, open the 16 ounce package of shredded xxxxx and dump it into the bowl (or rusty bucket). NOW IS THE TIME TO

STIR THE INGREDIENTS! Stir the ingredients exactly 28 times in a clockwise rotation.

The next step is critical to the flavor of your taco salad. You must butcher a cow and make hamburger (or buy it at the store if you want to speed the process) Brown the hamburger in an ordinary skillet on the stove for the amount of time it takes to read through the IRS tax code manual. Drain it and add it to the bowl (bucket). On occasion I have used other meat. For example, one of my friends prefers turkey. I don't use turkey when I make it for her, but I use faded beef and she never knows the difference. Follow the same steps as if using hamburger but skip section 7249.1456 on page 947 of the tax manual (this will save you 1.16 seconds) Another animal to try is the male offspring of a middle-age red-eyed, black-throated, Basilisk lizard from the north side of Mt. Everest. Dice the lizard and fry it in the leftover Kearney's 50 weight motor oil for three or four days until the stench dissipates. Once your choice of meat is prepared, throw it away because you are making vegetarian taco salad.

The next step involves choosing the lettuce. In the early days of the 14th Chin Dynasty I used head lettuce but have learned that romaine lasts longer and tastes better. Cut the romaine into 2 inch squares (plus or minus 34 microns) using an ordinary Samurai sword from 1376 (swords made from 1377 and later do not have the correct proportion of steel to Charmin bath tissue) Add the romaine squares one at a time. Then use a cement mixer to grind the sand and four pieces of gravel---- Ooops! Sorry that's the recipe for building roads in Northern Illinois--- Stir the taco salad ingredients again as many times as it takes to get a good burn in your biceps.

Congratulations! You have arrived at the final 438 steps.

To save time skip to step 437. It's time to add the dressing. The only dressing I recommend is xxxx xx xxxxxx xxx xxxxxxx. Add the entire bottle and using your fifty-year-old Brady-Welker slotted spoon, stir the taco salad once. Voila! You have done it! Simply store the taco salad in an underground bunker for 241 years, or until politicians place the country's needs above their own, whichever comes first (My wife made me include that part)

33

Remove the taco salad, using the same B-W slotted spoon and place it in 7.348 inch diameter ceramic bowls made by the ancestors of some long extinct sober Irish plumbers apprentices, sit at the Sigillaria wood butcher block island, turn on your TV and watch reruns of the Burns & Carson Show and relax. You are about to taste the world's best... Sorry again. I have been informed by the government that the phrase 'taco salad' has been deemed a national security risk. It must now be called xxxx xx x xxxxxx.

When your great-great-great grandchildren taste your taco salad, they will thank you profusely or I will personally refund your money up to the total of .000000016 cents.

A Treasure in the Attic

I was talking on the phone last week to my cousin Carl Horner because it was his birthday. We only talk on the phone a couple times a year, but when we do connect the calls last until our cell phone batteries run out. He and his wife live in Leakey Springs, Texas. I moved to Kinmundy Junction in southern Illinois after high school, but as kids we lived in Roarin' Plains, Texas. We went to high school there and would often stay at our great-grandma's ranch outside of town. That's where my grandpa and his grandma grew up.

As per norm, we ended up reminiscing about our grandparents and great-grandparents. Carl is my second cousin because his grandma and my grandpa were brother and sister, but he's closer than my other cousins. Anyway, we talked about some of the stories told at the round maple supper table in the dining room of the old ranch for fifty years or more. After going through all those tales, the conversation lagged for a moment. Then I thought about something that occurred when Carl and I were young teenagers in the early 50s.

"Do you remember that time out at the ranch when my grandma asked us to clean out that back corner of the attic?" I asked.

Carl wasn't sure what I meant, so I explained more.

"It was summer and we were staying at the ranch helping Grandma clean up around the yard and the attic."

"Was that the summer after your grandfather passed away?"

"I think so. He died the previous fall if I remember right. Grandma wanted to get rid of some of the stuff in the attic."

"I remember the attic. To get there you had to go in your grandmother's bedroom and there was a door in the corner."

"Yes! You had to pull that dresser out to get to it, and then there were these narrow stairs going up to the attic."

Carl laughed and added, "I remember that old cardboard box of marbles on the stairs. Do you remember that?"

I laughed and said, "Grandma didn't usually let us play with

35

them. I think they belonged to Grandpa. He collected them or something."

"Yeah, and I remember one time we were playing with them in front of the fireplace."

"Remember how the floor was slanted and the marbles always rolled toward the front of the house?" I asked interrupting him.

"I remember it now. I wonder whatever happened to them?"

"No clue, but I bet they'd be worth some money now. People will buy anything on eBay."

"So true. We were moving stuff around and found that old travel chest way back in the corner."

"Yeah, it was full of old books and a few other things," I said.

"Hey! Do you still have that old bullet and the badge?" Carl asked.

"I sure do. I keep them in the safety deposit box."

"Did you ever find out if that bullet was real silver?"

"No, but if it is, it would be worth a bundle. But I'd rather keep it as a souvenir."

"What about the books? Do you still have them?"

"Which ones?" I asked though I knew exactly which ones he meant.

"You know. The ones about our grandpas."

"They're on a shelf in my office right next to my desk."

"The one where you stare out the window at the birdbath and write those stories?"

"What can I say. I like watching the birds, Our cat even likes to get a drink from there. I'm sitting there now."

"Did you ever read any of them? The old books not your stories."

"When I was a kid I did, but I'd be afraid to open them now. They're pretty fragile."

"I remember when my grandfather and yours would get together. They'd set on the front porch out there at the ranch and tell us kids those old stories about when they were young."

"I used to sit there and just watch him talk and then twist

that old white mustache. That thing was so pointed I bet he could stab someone in the eye with it."

"Your grandpa would laugh and carry on. Sometimes it was hard to understand them when they'd use that old cowboy dialect."

"I loved to hear them talk about the outlaws they'd chase. They would use those colorful descriptions and all."

"I loved how every horse he ever rode on the job was named Horse," Carl said and then laughed until our sides hurt.

"I still have those cowboys hats," I said softly.

"Get out of the county!" Carl replied. "No way!"

I nodded and said, "Way."

"One of them had a bullet hole in it, right?"

"The black one your grandfather wore. He said it happened just after he bought it. He used to claim some Native American shot it."

"They used to come up with the craziest stories about the Indians... excuse me Native Americans," Carl said.

"I loved the names they gave to the outlaws."

"Do you have any idea how long they were Texas Rangers?" Carl asked.

"Grandpa used to claim it was for forty years, but Aunt Clara, your grandma, would shake her head and say it was more like twenty at most."

"I'd like to read those old paperbacks someday before I get too old to see clearly. Do you think someone will ever republish them?"

"I suppose it's possible. If I remember right... Well, let me see." I leaned over and looked at the bookcase and counted. "I have five books. I don't know if there were others or not."

"I remember when we carried that old trunk out of the attic. We brought it out to the porch and your grandma was sitting in her rocker. You held up one of the books and she sorta got all emotional."

"Yeah, she was still missing Grandpa a lot."

"I remember the titles were all about this adventure or that one and the good guys always captured the bad guys."

"Some of those old towns don't exist anymore."

"Leakey Springs is almost a ghost town now. The only business left is the gas station general store combo that the Polanka family runs.

I laughed and brought up something about the old books. "Do you remember Grandpa explaining how the publisher made the author change the names?"

"Yeah, I do. Instead of Clayton Horner my grandpa became Clay Horn."

"And instead of Adolph Tockstein my grandpa became Rex Ford. At least Clay Horn is close to your grandpa's name."

"They used to swear at that publisher for doing that."

"Yeah, he claimed their real names wouldn't fit on the cover."

"You have to admit the names he chose were purty catchy," Carl said.

"I reckon so," I added.

The Apolitical Blues, Part II

My wife and I were discussing Presidents a few days ago after the November election which resulted in a tie. I was mildly amused by the decision of both candidates to alternate weeks leading the country. I failed to see the benefit to such an arrangement while she praised the men for their willingness to reach a compromise beneficial to all politicians.

I told her such an abomination would have never occurred during the reign of my favorite president, Millard Fillmore. She laughed and refused to believe there had ever been a president named Millard Fillmore. She said it was a conspiracy of the Labor Party to subdue and repress the middle class. I used Wikipedia to show her a list of all U.S. Presidents. She reminded me Wikipedia can be edited by any first grader with a Smartphone and a set of Pokeman cards.

I asked her who she thought were the top ten presidents in history. She thought about it and suggested we make a list in secret and then announce our choices on our new YouTube reality show which had in three short weeks amassed a total of 26 subscribers. I agreed.

We retreated to our rooms and I began working on my list. I printed a list of all the presidents to date. I even included David Rice Atchison. The top position was simple. No one came close to topping President Fillmore. I read the list of former presidents and tried to think of the strong points of each one's administration. I quickly added Washington and Lincoln to my list. James Polk was another obvious choice. I immediately crossed out Hillary and Bill Clinton because I had never read any of their books. I eliminated Martin Van Buren, John Adams and John Quincy Adams because they were mostly bald and I had never voted for a partially bald man (or woman) for president. I took a serious look at Grover Cleveland, but finally decided he had enough hair on top of his head to avoid immediate disqualification.

Theodore Roosevelt made the cut because I like to visit National Parks. Calvin Coolidge was penciled in because of his eloquence as an orator. Thomas Jefferson made the top ten because in the photo on Wikipedia he had a curious smirk. I also chose him because he mentioned he had read all 27 of my books. I wonder which two he hadn't read.

I eliminated most of the recent commanders-in-chief because the verdict is still out on them. Harry Truman was a tough choice, but I crossed him off the list because I heard a rumor he was a Chicago Subs fan. Plus, there are still two members on the Supreme Court who were appointed by good ole Harry. There has been recent speculation both of these lifetime appointees have been dead for years, but no one has the courage to ask them if there are indeed still breathing. I smacked my forehead for not immediately including Richard Milhous Nixon (simply because of his middle name) and Rutherford B. Hayes (for his first name).

I counted the names I had chosen. Fillmore, Washington, Lincoln, Jefferson, Polk, Teddy Roosevelt, Coolidge, Nixon and Hayes. One more lucky man would make the list. I started the process of elimination. Woodrow Wilson was eliminated because I favor Brown University over Princeton. Harding, both Harrisons were crossed off. *Tippicanoe and Tyler, Too* was the worst campaign slogan of all time. John Tyler was scratched, as though he ever had a chance. Ha!

I admit I struggled for minutes to add the tenth man to my list. Then I had an epiphany, or the hiccups. I couldn't tell which. The Seattle Seahawks are famous for their 12th man. I decided to add three more names to my list. It was my reality show, so I could do as I pleased. As long as those 26 subscribers didn't object. FDR was added because he was the closest thing to a lifer president we've had. Lyndon B. Johnson is the definition of a politician so he was added. One more. I looked at the photos again. I shook my head as I read through the list. No one seemed deserving of the coveted twelfth spot. Finally, one name jumped out at me. Aha! How could I not include the only man who served as our country's leader without ever being elected to the office. Gerald R. Ford. The only negative thing I could think of was the fact he played football for the University of Michigan. Being a lifelong Notre Dame fan, I decided I could not choose a Wolverine. I quickly added Ronald

Reagan because he was born in Illinois and I liked his movies.

My list was complete. I smirked because there was no way my wife could top my list. She would probably choose leaders who married good-looking women or lowered taxes or created extra jobs. No such superficial criteria for me.

Four Letter Words

I have tried as an author to limit my use of four letter words. I believe for the most part they are unnecessary. However, I admit to using two of them far too often. They don't add anything to my stories and usually only distract the reader. Those words are 'that' and 'just.' (I would add 'very' to this list as well.) I'll give you some examples from the first Emmy book.

"I heard Daddy tell Mommy that we might move again this summer.

Grandpa knew that Raymond and Patricia had probably lived in ten other neighborhoods through the years before the girls were born.

There used to be a farm just over there, Emmy."

"I was just showing Grandma the backyard. I wasn't really going to jump down," Emmy explained.

She feared that her father and grandfather would get so upset with each other that she would not be allowed to see her grandfather and grandmother.

If those offending four letter words are just eliminated from the sentences, the meaning doesn't change all that very much. The reader can still understand the lines. You may argue that these words just take up a small amount of space on the page, but that just isn't necessarily true. For instance, if I were to eliminate those two words that aren't very necessary from my first manuscript, it would shorten the novel by eighteen pages. That is a significant amount. Just think of the very consequential reduced printing cost. If all writers were to eliminate gratuitous four letter words, we could save hundreds of trees every year.

Granted, there are instances when these words are just useful and very much needed to add tension that increases the drama. That I can justify. However, too often I find myself reading a novel with superfluous use of unnecessary four letter words just because the author doesn't know that the words can very easily be eliminated just by reading through the lines that contain them.

I have learned to search through my books and short stories to eliminate those words just as often as that is possible. It's true that they can't be eliminated completely. That just doesn't work and could very easily confuse the reader. Hopefully, over the years my 'skill' as a writer has improved to the point where I can just eliminate those words that just don't add very much value to my work.

Thank you for listening to my rant about four letter words. I promise that I will do just about everything in my power to not bore the reader with four letter words in the very near future.

The St. Louis Cardinals Should Change Their Name, Part 2

Another hero of my youth is gone. Bob Gibson, the fiercest pitcher I can remember, passed away in his hometown of Omaha on October 2. He was 84. During the 60s Gibson was known for intimidating opposing players. It was an era when pitchers could throw inside and back a batter off the plate. Today it would not be allowed. Gibson was more than a baseball player. He played basketball for the Harlem Globetrotters and starred at Creighton University, too. Besides being an amazing pitcher, he was a good hitter once batting over 300 for the year. In those days, pitchers came to the plate to hit.

The Cardinals of the 60s were a racially mixed team. There were whites, African Americans and Hispanics in the lineup. Gibson was a man who did not tolerate racial prejudice and led the cause for equality in housing and other issues. He was also known for not talking to opposing players on the field when he was in the game. He might not have even talked to his teammates.

In 1968 Gibson had an ERA of 1.12. That was the lowest since the dead-ball era at the turn of the century. He completed 28 of the 34 games he started. Pitchers now rarely pitch a complete game. Pitch counts and computers rule today's game. In game 1 of the 1968 World Series Gibson struck out 17 Detroit Tigers breaking a record.

Another Hall of Fame Cardinal, Lou Brock, passed away on September 6th of this year. He was a valuable members of the Cardinals dynasty. Cardinal fans can thank the Chicago Subs for that. Brock was traded to the Cardinals for Ernie Broglio, who had a couple good years for the Cardinals, but never panned out for the Subs. Brock was known for his ability to steal bases and ended his career with over 3,000 hits.

My favorite Cardinal in my youth was Ken Boyer, who played third base. I had a Ken Boyer glove, and I think I used a Ken Boyer model bat in Little League. Sadly, he passed away from cancer at the age of 51 in 1982.

Another Cardinal, Curt Flood, is known as the player who helped create free agency. He fought the system and won. Players today should be thankful.

I did a search on Wikipedia and found that many of the star players from the 60s Cardinals are gone. Bill White, Dick Groat, Julian Javier, Orlando Cepeda, Mike Shannon and Tim McCarver are still around. Shannon and McCarver are broadcasters. FYI, Bob Uecker was a member of the Cardinals in 1964 and 1965. Fans who don't remember Uecker as a player or broadcaster may remember him from the movies *Major League* and *Major League II* where he appeared as a broadcaster alongside Skip Griparis. There might be a link between long life and broadcasting baseball games.

Another favorite Cardinal of the 50s and 60s, and member of baseball's Hall of Fame, was Albert 'Red' Schoendienst. Red was born on Germantown, Illinois, in 1923. With a name like Schoendienst, where else should he be born. He played for and managed the Cardinals for many years. He took over as manager in 1965 and stayed in that position until 1976. He wore a baseball uniform as either a player, coach or manager for 74 consecutive years. He passed away in 2018 at the age of 95.

The man most identified as a Cardinal was Stan 'The Man' Musial. There is a statue of him outside the stadium. Must be where the Bulls got the idea. Musial started his major league career on September 17, 1941. No, Tom Hernandez, I was not at the game. Anyone who knows anything about baseball has heard of Stan Musial. If you haven't, you aren't a real fan. Look him up. His career stats are amazing. He retired in 1963, and still holds some records. I watched his final game on TV. I can't remember if I skipped school or not. In those days few Cardinal games were broadcast on television, and never a home game. They made an exception for Musial's last game. He got a hit in his last at bat and then was taken out of the game. Musial was a rarity. He was a genuinely gracious and humble man. He was known for his humor and ability to play the harmonica. He was married to his high school sweetheart for 72 years and never once cheated on his income taxes.

My father and his twin brother moved to Granite City while in high school. They would take the bus or train across the Mississippi River into St. Louis and go to Cardinal games at what was then called Sportsman Park. When I was a kid, my father often took me and my cousin Paul to games at the same stadium now called Busch Stadium. It is the stadium pictured on the pennant hanging on the wall behind me. I would show you, but I did that in Part 1. Paul and I would often wait outside the door the players exited and ask for autographs. Some players would sign. Others would ignore us. On one of those occasions I got Stan Musial's autograph on a scorecard. I still have the old scorecard. It and several others from the era are sitting on a table under the Cardinal pennant. If the house ever changes on fire, I will grab the pennant, the scorecards and several thumb drives before I race out of the house. The thumb drives are my backups for all my writing and photos of grandkids. Oh, I might warn my wife about the fire, also.

The Typewriter Virus, Part 2

Ah! Remember the old days? Back when life was much simpler. Back before we had cell phones, iPads, cars that drove themselves and wristwatches that connected to the Internet and worlds far beyond our galaxy. Okay, maybe they are limited to this galaxy, but who knows how long that will be. Of course, if you are under the age of forty, or so, you don't remember what it was like not to have all this technology. Today, even the most primitive natives deep in the Amazon rain forest are capable of ordering their daily needs from Amazon.

As a child I remember rotating the TV antenna (not the rabbit ears that sat on the TV but the tall antenna outside the house) to allow for the best reception of all three available channels. Would you believe TV stations shut down at night? True story! I remember sharing our telephone line with other parties. At least we had a telephone and indoor plumbing. Many of my older relatives would share stories of how they came to this country from Europe along with Christopher Columbus, Henry Hudson (who later started his own automobile manufacturing company) Francis Drake, Vasco de Gama, Ferdinand Magellan and probably the most famous explorer of all, Perkins MacGhee.

I wish I had written down more of those old tales. Imagine the thrill of crossing the Atlantic Ocean in a ship without any form of communication with civilization. No satellite phones. No wireless radio signals. Not even a carrier pigeon. Sometimes the journey would take an entire week. Ye gads! (Gadzooks, egad, the dickens you say, or some other colorful term inserted here). Picture spending an entire week living with strangers on a ship cruising aimlessly through uncharted waters. The courage of those early seafaring captains must have far exceeded that of Captain Stubing or even Jonas Grumby.

Now I freely admit I would miss my flip-phone, my computer with its whopping 10 megabytes of storage, my 15 inch, cathode ray tube computer monitor and my indispensable road maps, that I stuff in the trunk, for use on my journeys across the

Lincoln Highway. But I am spoiled. Ha! I've even heard of a company trying to develop an electric typewriter. How in the world would you use that if you had to move about the office or home? Such fanciful flights of fantasy. Alex Bell would roll over in his grave. Unless he was cremated. I wonder if anyone knows if he was.

But back to the typewriter virus. Where was I going with this? Yes, I remember now. The good old days. Back when you could eat at a restaurant and sit down, go to a store to buy groceries and not have to wait until an aisle was clear before entering, visit your local cinema and watch the cartoons before the double feature from the comfort of your '63 Chevy. Listen to Larry Lujack on WLS and laugh as he and Little Tommy discussed the Cheap Trashy Show Biz Report. Are there reruns of Captain Kangaroo on anymore? I hear people complaining about not be allowed to leave their homes. I grew up in a period of time when 99% of people never traveled more than five miles from where they were born on the farm and Mom would plow forty acres later that afternoon. Were people tougher then? Now kids complain if they have to walk down the block to wait for school bus. (Ooops! I forgot all schools are closed for the foreseeable future.) I know you have heard this one before and will roll your eyes because it's so cliché, but back when I went to school, we had to walk ten miles through three-foot deep snow (in the summer it rained ten inches a day) uphill both ways and even chop the firewood for the pot-bellied stove in the middle of our one-room schoolhouse. And we never complained!

I still have hopes things will return to a pre-typewriter-virus world, but in the meantime, I'm enjoying writing my serious, thought-provoking blogs (those never get posted just mindless stuff like this) and watching reruns of *The Many Loves of Dobie Gillis* and *You Bet Your Life*. One of these days I'm going to guess the secret woid.

Top Ten Things People Don't Know About Me

One of our recent assignments for WriteOn Joliet was to compile a list of ten things people don't know about you... me... whoever. I though I'd give it a shot. I will start at the beginning.

1. My mother was not present at my birth. She was a schoolteacher and was busy grading papers.
2. I never knew my paternal grandfather because he passed away in 1926.
3. My second grade teacher forced me to learn to write with my right hand instead of my preferred left. To this day I can still write with both hands (though usually not at the same time.)
4. I didn't know my name was Kenneth until I started first grade. I thought it was Kenny because that's what everyone called me. (We didn't have kindergarten in my hometown.)
5. I learned to fish at my grandfather's pond when I was a kid. Later, I learned it was easier to use a pole and not my hands.
6. During inclement weather, I would ride my bike in circles in our garage. I guess that explains why I'm so dizzy to this day.
7. I was 6-4 and weighed 140 pounds when I got married. When I turned sideways to face my wife to say my vows, no one could see me.
8. I played competitive basketball until I was 38. One league I played in contained ex-NBA players. I realized I was out of my element and took up bicycle racing.
9. I once rode my bike 177 miles in just over eight hours. Don't ask me why. I averaged 28.5 miles-per-hour in a criterium. I hit 57 mph going down a mountain road in Colorado, hit a pebble in the road, hopped the bike but didn't crash. (During one training ride in Colorado, my teammates and I passed all the motorized traffic on a winding downhill road. That was awesome.)

10. I appeared on TV numerous times as the drummer for a famous band in the 70s. (Extra credit for correctly guessing the band's name.)
11. One of my father's ancestors fought in the Revolutionary War. (I don't know which side he fought for, though.)
12. I can count past ten.
13. Xxxx
14. I'm superstitious. (Not really.)
15. I've written 25, no, 26 books. (If you read this after June 2020 it will be 27 books. Maybe 28.)
16. Each book has sold at least one copy. (Thank you, Andy.)
17. "He moved with the agility of a brontosaurus in heat as he slipped under the shiny, satin sheet next to her." is the most frequently quoted line from my writing.

The TV Westerns of My Youth, Part 2

The fifth essential part of any good Western was the fistfight. Muhammad Ali and Joe Frazier were lightweights compared to the pugilistic encounters in every episode of most Westerns. Though the fistfights occurred less often in *The Lone Ranger.* Of course, Roy and Gene would sing a song immediately after going fifteen rounds with the villain. Not a hair would be out of place and clothes would be clean seconds after the combatants flung each other around in the dust and dirt of the desert. One exception to this rule happened in a movie where the action took place in a mudhole at the bottom of the hill. Wait! That was in a John Wayne movie, so it doesn't count. Western movies didn't follow the same rules and time restrictions as the TV shows. They also had to reload their guns after firing only a few hundred rounds.

The sixth essential part of any good Western would be the writers. The script writers should not be neglected or forgotten. The skill to create a totally unique thirty minute episode each week with all the required changes in names and sometimes even wardrobe and locations, certainly must have taxed the creativity of the third-grade writers employed by the studios. One scene in The Cisco Kid occurred in the same set of rocks and the villains wore the same shirts even though the locations were supposed to be on opposite sides of the state. Okay, there were plot holes bigger than the Eisenhower Tunnel on Interstate 70 in Colorado, but who cared. It was more important to catch the bad guys.

Seventh. I have never encountered a dishonest attorney in real life, but in the Westerns of my youth, all the attorneys were more corrupt than today's politicians. They would scheme to cheat the honest ranchers and farm owners, who were struggling to eke out a living. The crooked shysters would try to steal land, cattle, goats, sheep, pots and pans and anything else worth more than a plug nickel. (I do not believe all politicians are corrupt, dishonest or immoral. Hopefully, I won't be sued by the hundreds of out of work attorneys who read my blogs religiously.)

The music played an equally important role in the shows. Perhaps second only to the horses and occasional pet dog. Not only was the theme song catchy and memorable, but the music would add suspense, tension and sorely needed drama to each scene. Unless it was Pancho. Leo Carrillo, who played Pancho, was famous for his mangling of the English language though he was a university graduate and 70 years old when *The Cisco Kid* began. Can you imagine a chase scene without the music galloping along with the thunderous hoofbeats of the mighty steeds? Nor can I.

Life was different in the 50s. Cars had huge fins. They were manufactured in Detroit out of real American steel and weighed more than modern tanks. TVs were pieces of furniture, and if you had enough money to buy one, broadcast shows in color, which didn't matter for most kids Westerns. Only *The Cisco Kid* was filmed in color (To the best of my knowledge. Maybe later versions of The Lone Ranger were in color, but it didn't matter as long as they didn't change the theme music.) TV stations shut down at night, and in my hometown, whenever the wind blew too hard or the cloud cover was too thick. Sex did not take place in Westerns, or any other network show, because even married couples slept in different beds. (Watch the Dick Van Dyke Show.) Thus the twenty year gap in which no children were born in the US.

Perhaps Westerns will make a comeback. I would watch them if they did. How old would Clayton Moore be now? Could he still ride a horse up and down vertical hills? And wouldn't the world benefit from a new version of "Hi-Yo, Silver. Away!" (Just don't mess with the William Tell Overture theme.)

Swish! Nothing But Net

Only seconds remained on the clock, and the crowd in the New Orleans Superdome was absolutely silent as the tense game neared its climax. LeBron James, Jr was at the line for a free throw that would ice the game. He bounced the ball twice before eyeing the basket and releasing it. The ball hit the back of the rim and bounced high in the air twice before slipping off of the cylinder. Benjamin McGee grabbed the rebound, dribbled the length of the court, faked out five defenders, rose high in the air and flipped the ball toward the basket a split-second before the buzzer sounded. SWISH! NOTHING BUT NET! The crowd of 75,000 now-screaming fans roared louder than a dozen jet engines and actually shook the building. The Plainfield University Green Avengers won the 2033 NCAA World Championship. His teammates carried him off the court on their shoulders before the crowd could surround them...

Okay, that's not exactly the way it happened, but a proud grandfather can dream, right?

Several months ago, Grandma signed Ben up for a Plainfield Park District basketball league for first-graders. The team practiced a few times and then the season began. We attended Ben's games and supported him as only proud grandparents can. The team won a few games and lost a few. Ben didn't mind as long as there were snacks after the game. Ben was not the most talented player on the team, but he did try hard. Only a few of the eight players on the team could even dribble the ball. Having never played basketball before, or any other sport, he didn't quite understand the difference between offense and defense. He would guard his man all over the court regardless of which team had the ball. Many times the ball would be close to Ben without him realizing it. Sometimes he reached out tentatively to grab the ball, but more aggressive kids would snatch it away. Sometimes Ben would touch the ball during the game, other times he wouldn't. I think he might have taken a couple shots during the season, but none came anywhere close to the basket.

Because of the Coronavirus pandemic the season was cut short. Ben's last game would be March 14. We sat on the cold, metal chairs along the side of the gym to watch. Only four players from Ben's team were able to play. That meant Ben would have to play the entire game and Grandma and Brandy were afraid he would get worn out. I was hoping Ben would have a chance to shoot the ball and make a basket since this would be the final game. Early in the first half, Ben was surrounded by players but was able to get a shot off. It missed everything and we sighed forlornly. In the second half, he had another chance. He dribbled to a position close to the basket and with the other players out of position, he was able to get off a clean shot. It banked off the backboard and dropped cleanly through the net. Ben made a basket!!! I think everyone in the gym cheered for him. He was grinning as he trotted to the other end of the court. I was so happy for him.

I heard Brandy (Ben's mom) telling Kevin (Ben's father and my son) about the basket on her cell phone. She told him I had tears in my eyes because Ben had made a basket. What?!?! How ridiculous! No way would I get emotional about a silly basketball game between a bunch of first-graders. It must have been a speck of dust under the contacts I no longer wear that caused my eyes to appear wet. Yeah! That's it. It was a gigantic piece of dirt that caused my eyes to erroneously appear to fill with tears. Yeah! That's my story and I'm sticking to it. Lots of dust in that gym. Just ask any of the other grandparents who were there. Tears? No chance.

The St. Louis Cardinals Should Change Their Name, Part 3

Though the Cardinals won their eighth consecutive World Series title by sweeping the Mexico City Vaqueros and outscoring them by a combined score of 48-3, the lopsided series was watched by record crowds on black and white televisions around the globe. All major television networks covered the series, played in relative isolation on an uneven grass and mud surface behind a barn in an area previously used to hold rock festivals on Max Yasgur's farm in upstate New York. Some networks used multiple cameras, special announcers and special effects to create virtual crowds approaching a million people.

The combined efforts of league commissioners from all major sports was widely attributed by sportswriters, pizza delivery boys, casual fans and Marge and Art at Frank's Diner in revitalizing fan interest in professional sports after a two-decade long season of apathy. The now nearly forgotten pandemic of 2020 which started the public's indifference toward sports, organized religion and barbers with the name Terence was rarely mentioned by five-term president Joe Walsh.

Grand Supreme President Walsh, whose initial suggestion of having all sports teams dress up as their team nicknames was met with scorn and derision, had the last laugh. After attendance skyrocketed to nearly a hundred people per event, politicians, late night television hosts and out of work teaching assistants around the globe were claiming the idea as their own.

For several teams the switch in uniforms was relatively easy. The Cardinals, Orioles, Hawks, Eagles, Blue Jays and other teams named for birds, simply added feather to their uniforms. The Pirates and Buccaneers were handicapped by their eye patch and several members of the team were injured when they tripped over their swords. Other teams struggled to maintain a high level of athleticism. The Dolphins tried in vain to use their flippers to catch the football. The Marlins suffered much the same fate. The San Francisco Giants found using stilts slowed them too much and

55

changed their name to the Average-Sized-Humans, but league commissioner Benjamin McGee vetoed the change. The Indians, Braves, Warriors, Chiefs and Redskins were allowed to ride horses and shoot the opposition with bows and arrows. Teams were often decimated after these games. The Cowboys and Texas Rangers rode the Colts and Broncos into the ground.

The Miami Heat withered midway through the year. The Orlando Magic and Washington Wizards would disappear at times in the middle of games. The Charlotte Hornets buzzed about in their new uniforms to all who would listen but were swatted away by the Nets. The Grizzlies, Timberwolves, Bears, Panthers and other teams soon learned to run on all fours.

The Saints, Angels and Padres were blessed by new talent. The Utah Jazz played well, but struggled with following set guidelines. The 49ers found new Nuggets when Joe Montana came out of retirement, but were buried under an Avalanche of Maple Leafs in the Rockies. The Predators, Coyotes and Sharks feasted on weaker teams like the Ducks, Penguins, Pelicans and Cubs. The LA Lakers and Clippers floundered in a rough sea of turbulent waves caused by the Thunder, Lightning and Hurricanes. Interest sparked by Lebron James, playing in his tenth season for both LA teams simultaneously, reached an all-time zenith when the Lakers played the Clippers on Christmas Day. James guarding himself scored a record 137 points and blocked his own shots 18 times in the game before taking himself out of both lineups due to exhaustion and old age.

The Kings, Royals and Senators played as though they were above the laws of the game and created new Bills to suit their needs. Emperor Walsh signed a decree that expanded the new uniform craze to include minor leagues as well as the majors. Players for the Biscuits, Skeeters, Canaries, Milkmen, Poodles and Jumbo Shrimp began a petition to boycott the season unless the Goats and Flying Squirrels were excluded from the new directive.

Will professional sports on any level ever regain the mystic and allure they enjoyed in the heydays of Jordan, Manning, Brady, Trubisky, Ruth, Gehrig and Valmy Thomas, or is that era lost forever to the Sounds of Wind Surges and the rattling of Sabres?

I Forgive You, Don Denkinger

Saturday, October 26, 1985 7:25 pm (CT) at Royals Stadium in Kansas City, Missouri, a date and time which, to steal the words of FDR, will live in infamy. At least in the hearts and memories of Cardinal fans.

Allow me to set the scene in case there might be one person out there unaware of this tragic event. Game six of the World Series between the perennial winners the St. Louis Cardinals and the upstart Kansas City Royals was, to say the least, a pitcher's duel. The score was 1-0 in favor of the heavy fan favorite Cardinals going into the bottom of the ninth. Cardinals manager, Dorrel Norman Elvert Herzog, better known as "Whitey," from New Athens, Illinois, brought in rookie reliever Todd Worrell to close out the game... and he would have if not for a series of unfortunate events. A series of events strange enough to have been made into book fourteen of the set by author Daniel Handler.

You may ask, "Who is Don Denkinger and how does he fit into the series of unfortunate events?"

I will explain. Denkinger (insert extraneous biographical information here*) was the crew chief and working as the first base umpire on the night of this infamous event. The first batter of the inning, pinch-hitter Jorge Orta, chopped a ball to the right of first baseman Jack Clark, whose normal position was in right field. Clark fielded the ball and flipped it to Worrell covering first base. The ball clearly beat the runner to the bag. Everyone in the stadium could see it. My great-grandmother who was legally blind could see it. Stevie Wonder, Ray Charles and Helen Keller saw the play and agreed the runner should have been called out. Peter Ueberroth, the commissioner of MLB, was in attendance and (most likely**) gasped at the blown call.

Everyone knows what happened next, so I will not go over the details etched in the mind of even the most casual fan of baseball. People who would not normally watch an inning of baseball, people who would rather have their eyes poked by a dull needle, people who... I apologize. I was getting carried away. My point is if you ask ten million people in Wuhan, China, who won the 1985 World Series, 99.9999% of them will say the Cardinals were robbed. (They can also tell you the price of tea.)

Am I bitter toward Don Denkinger? Not after 36 years. If he lived next door would I engage in small talk about baseball with him? Never. Denkinger is human. He made an error in judgment. Unfortunately for him it was seen by billions of Cardinal fans all over the galaxy. I will never forget how a series of unfortunate events robbed the Cardinals of a well-deserved World Series title, but I forgive him.

** I was not sitting next to Ueberroth, but persistent rumors over the years claim he gasped audibly at the blown call and whispered these words, "The Cardinals were robbed!" Just a rumor!

* I omitted the extraneous biographical information because Denkinger is still alive and no doubt the subject of scorn from baseball fans from all over the world. I did not want to enable people to keep piling on the abuse. After all, I forgive him.

The Past Is Now The Future, Or Is It The Other Way Around?

When I began writing my Emmy Stories almost ten years ago. I set the stories in the past. My main character, Emmy Colasanti, was born in 1980. She was four-years-old in the prologue of the first book. She grew up quickly in that first book. She graduated from high school and even moved into her first apartment by the end.

Since that time I have written sixteen other books about Emmy, her family, friends, foes and whoever I could create. She went through struggles, moments of great happiness and other moment of pure boredom called everyday life. She got married, had kids, started one career, ended that and launched a new career as a writer. (I get some of my best plot lines from Emmy, but since I created her, she can't sue me for plagiarism)

Now I face a dilemma, time has caught up to her world. I am now writing in the present. The eighteenth book in the series starts on Christmas Day of 2019 which then leads into 2020, and unless you've been living in a cave without LG5 or whatever technology is current, or in New Kinmundy, Alaska, for the last decade, you know the world has changed drastically since January. No longer can I research things on Wikipedia because the events of May, June and July (when this book ends) haven't happened yet. No one knows with any degree of certainty when life will return to those thrilling days of yesteryear. (That's a shameless plug for my new book *The Amazing Adventures of Rex Ford & Clay Horn.*)

I am now faced with something I've never encountered in all the years of writing about Emmy, Kenny, Tony, Kristen and all the characters listed in the fifty page document I use to keep track of details like who was born when, where they lived, what kind of car they drive and whether or not they floss daily. Now I am faced with an enemy no one can defeat. Time. Or patience or something along those lines. I have reached out to friends who deal with our new reality on a daily basis, but even they cannot predict the future. I want to keep writing and finish this story, but I can't. What if something totally crazy happens in late June, and I don't include it in my book. Sure, I write fiction and I can take liberties with the real world. However, I do want to portray a feasible reality for my imperfect characters.

What to do? Should I turn my attention to *More Adventures of Rex Ford & Clay Horn* (another plug. I already have the cover designed) or should I be patient until July 8 when Emmy turns forty, which happens at the end of the book. Many times I write the last chapter near the beginning... You know what I mean. Holy Cow! Is it possible Little Emmy is that old? Where has the time gone. She was just a child in... never mind.

I could concentrate on writing blogs that let my mind wander and where my imagination is given free reign. (You should read some of the stuff I write that my wife tells me to delete.) In the meantime, I will continue working on Emmy's Story, Part 17, thinking of creative ways for Rex and Clay to have one cliffhanging adventure after another and writing enough blogs to fill up my website.

"I Don't Want A Dead Bird!"

"'I don't want a dead bird,' your mother screamed," Kenny said with a laugh.

"What are you talking about?" Emmy asked walking through the kitchen with a basket of dirty clothes.

"I'm telling the kids about Mr. Souchek."

"Then you better tell them the whole story," she ordered.

"Okay, I will," Kenny said. "It happened like this..."

"Emmy, this letter came in the mail today for you. It's from the office of Bushell, Strohmeyer and Plimpton. They must be attorneys," Kenny said. He handed the letter to Emmy as she walked into the kitchen.

"What could this be about? I hope we're not being sued or something."

"I think the only way to find out is to open it," Kenny suggested.

Emmy opened the letter and they read it together.

"I haven't thought about Mr. Souchek for several years. He was the old man who lived next door when I was a little girl. He and his wife treated me like a grandchild."

"I vaguely remember the name."

"He passed away at least five or six years ago."

"Why would this attorney need to see you in his office as soon as convenient?" Kenny asked.

"I have no idea, but maybe we should call this number."

They did and set up an appointment for the next morning. They drove to downtown SoHam, found the office in the old Palace Theater Building, and were shown into Mike Bushell's office.

"Now I know why I thought I recognized the name," Emmy said. "My friend Annie O'Dell used to work for you."

"She did. Now I handle her writing career. The legal side of it."

He offered coffee, which they declined, and they talked

about Annie, her family and her books for a time.

"I know you must be curious about the letter."

"Yes, we couldn't fathom why Mr. Souchek would instruct you to contact us. All I could think it might be about was the old doll his wife gave me years ago. I still have it, if I need to give it back. She said it was the only doll she had growing up during the depression."

"It's not about a doll, Mrs. Colwell."

"You better call her Emmy," Kenny said. "She might sue you otherwise."

"All right. Emmy it is. Mr. Souchek passed away in 2004. Six years ago plus a couple months. His will stated his estate be divided among any living relatives on his side of the family who could prove kinship. He specified a time limit of five years. That limit passed, and the estate was probated..."

Emmy listened as Mr. Bushell explained all the legalities involved with closing the estate.

"So each of the relatives received a check for $1,127.19. This is the judge's signature to close the estate. Only one thing remains. Actually two items. He very specifically bestowed two items to be held in safe keeping until such time as required... blah, blah, blah. There is the automobile that had been stored in his garage and a birdcage."

"A birdcage!" Emmy and Kenny said together.

"Do you remember anything about a car?" Mr. Bushell asked.

"I know he drove a beat up old Ford. Why would he leave that to me?"

"It wasn't an old Ford." He showed Emmy a photograph of Mr. Souchek's garage. "Can you make out the tarp behind all the junk?"

"Yeah! He used to brag about some fancy old car under it. I peeked under the tarp one day, and it was just a piece of junk like all the other stuff around it."

Mr. Bushell shook his head.

"Em, I think Mr. Bushell is trying to tell you something."

"What? It wasn't just a piece of junk?"

Mr. Bushell held up a piece of paper. "This is the title to that piece of junk. It's actually a 1958 Packard Hawk with a supercharged V8 engine."

Kenny gasped and held his breath.

Emmy shrugged. "What does that mean? Is it mine? Does it even run?"

"It runs and it belongs to you. I can have it appraised if you'd like."

"No, if Mr. Souchek wanted me to have it, I'll keep it out of respect."

"That leaves the birdcage," Mr. Bushell said.

"I remember he had songbirds in a cage, but they would die and he would replace them. He called each one Fortune and had them stuffed or whatever you call it. His wife always made fun of that."

"He left his 'Fortune' to you, Emmy."

"Get out! I don't want a dead bird!" she screamed.

"Unfortunately, or perhaps fortunately in this case, he didn't mean one of the birds. He meant the actual birdcage." He stood up, walked over to a large cabinet and pulled out an ordinary looking birdcage. "This is what he left you along with its contents."

"The contents better not be those stuffed birds."

"Mr. Souchek left detailed instructions about the cage itself. It was built with a false bottom just deep enough to place a letter passed down from his great-great grandfather."

"Are you saying the birdcage is an antique and worth some money?" Kenny asked.

Mr. Bushell shook his head. "No, the cage isn't worth more than a few dollars. However, I have a copy of a letter contained in the birdcage. The original letter is in a safe place to keep it from disintegrating." He waved his hand. "It's been authenticated by experts in that field and is kept in a secure place. This is the copy." He slid the letter across the table.

Emmy and Kenny peered closely at the letter. They read part of it.

Kenny looked up and said, "It's reads like some kind of legal document. It's all legalese to me."

63

"Me, too," Emmy added. "There's a signature at the bottom. It's hard to make out, but it looks like an A followed by a name."

Kenny realized it first, grabbed the copy and took a closer look. "It says Lincoln, Em. A Lincoln."

"You mean like Abraham Lincoln? The President?"

Mr. Bushell smiled. "The letter is dated February of 1840 which makes it one of the oldest, if not the oldest, known signature of President Lincoln."

"That must be worth more than a birdcage," Emmy said.

Kenny rolled his eyes and Mr. Bushell nearly choked.

To ? or Not To ? That Is the ?

I'm paraphrasing Hamlet of course. Shakespeare in case no one reads his stories anymore. I was never much of a fan because he didn't write about sports, but I digress. Before you move to the next website, this is not about Shakespeare. I will try not to bore thee with flowery prose like 'A rose by any other name.' Whatever! I mean go hang out in a convent, Shakespeare.

This is a short discourse about grammar. Not the actor, but commas and periods and exclamation points and those pesky little colons and semi-colons (which I rarely use because I don't know the difference between the two:). Listen up! I'm not going to praise William Bullokar with platitudes, neither shall I bury him. For indeed grammar merely acquaints one's soul with misery and madness. In this winter of our discontent with social distancing, I beg to remind you all that glitters is not gold. In other words, I admit my limited knowledge of the correct use of grammar has hampered my writing at times. The fault lies not within the stars, but in myself. Perhaps, I didn't pay close enough attention in school, but, for my own part, grammar was Greek to me. (and I'm not talking about colons and semi-colons). There are so many rules and exceptions to the rules. More rules than there are things in heaven and earth in this infinite philosophy called English grammar. Thank you ever so much, William Bullokar.

I use my computer to write, and not having taken a typing class in fifty years (give or take – mostly give) I am not the best typist. When I get going, I speed along faster than a horse racing though its kingdom without a lot of thought to punctuation. I will often add a period to the end of a sentence simply to keep the momentum going. The course of correct grammar never did run smooth on my keyboard. This brings me to my point. I shall attempt to maintain brevity less I cause you to lose your wit. Though the better part of valor might be discretion, I must remain true to myself. Too often have I submitted a less-than-perfect manuscript to the valiant young lady who volunteered to read them. Liz Hubbell. Bless her heart for she the epitome of patience.

I am positive there were many times when she must have muttered 'Off with his head! His errors shall last for eternity.' If I ever got one sentence correct, it would lie buried with the dust of my bones. Alas and alack, she did not cry havoc and let loose the dogs of grammar war. Instead she exercised patience until at last the wheel has come full circle and I am now here. Ah, sigh no more, readers, sigh no more. I have seen better days!

For years I toiled miserably in the bottomless pit of the quagmire of grammar with no medicine but that of hope. However, action is eloquence, and now I have at least one foot on the shore while the other remains in the sea. Yea I have been to the feast of correct grammar and stolen the scraps that fell to the floor. To put it simply, I have sought the remedy and found it in such stuff as dreams are made on. Namely, GrammarBook.com. Upon discovering this magnificent pearl of the mind's eye, I am now able to add a question mark to the end of a sentence? (and sometimes, correctly). No longer shall I see grammar as a dagger before my eyes, but, as one who has died but one death in the eyes of my editor, I see it as a world stage upon which we the players playing our parts must make our entrances and exits.

I will not profess loudly like a cymbal clanging in the darkness of the constant moon, since nothing comes from nothing, but I revel in the books, the arts, the academies that show, contain, and nourish all the world's libraries. I have not conquered grammar with slings and arrows, but I have trapped it in my snares. Never again will I crown my head with uneasiness over a simple ellipses, but I shall forbid my eternal soul to be disparaged over what I may know, and delight in what I may become. I may never achieve the greatness of William Bullokar, but I may have competency thrust upon me. My heart yearns to peer through the window of the morning sun to learn what light doth shine through. To the ever-changing rules of grammar I say "Out you impediment to the true mind of the heart." I find my strength in this royal throne of kings, this sceptered bible... This blessed earth, this tome of knowledge... This English book – *The Blue Book of Grammar and Punctuation*. (by Jane Strauss)

Happy Birthday, Aunt Ann

Ann Tockstein Williams was born on April 25, 1920. Yes! I have the year correct. My aunt was born 100 years ago. There is a character in my books who lives to be 100, but I've never known someone in real life to make it that far. She is the first in our family!

My grandparents, Ann's mother and father, immigrated to this country from Europe like so many others did in the late nineteenth and twentieth centuries. They eventually met in Chicago, fell in love and got married. Uncle Adolph was born in Chicago, but then Grandpa Tockstein decided to buy a farm in Southern Illinois. Grandma didn't want to move, but she did. They bought 120 acres along the Patoka Road. (Sorry, but I can't call it the Kinoka Road.) Ann was born in 1920 followed by Uncle Charlie, my mom Elsie, and lastly by Uncle Bill.

1920! Wow! Just think. Ann, and her brothers and sisters, did not have iPhones, Internet, Netflix, Zoom or even McDonald's. They didn't have any kind of phone. No TV. Probably not even a radio. What did they do for entertainment? How could they survive? No unlimited texting! How prehistoric.

I researched notable news events of 1920 and came up with these.

Stan Musial was born. Woodrow Wilson was the president. Douglas Fairbanks married Mary Pickford. A Chicago grand jury convened to investigate charges that 8 White Sox players conspired to fix the 1919 World Series. The 6th Rose Bowl was played: Harvard beat Oregon 7-6. Boston Red Sox baseball club owner Harry Frazee announced agreement to sell slugger Babe Ruth to the New York Yankees for $125,000 in cash and a $350,000 loan; start of the 84 year "Curse of the Bambino." Novelist and short story writer F. Scott Fitzgerald (23) wed novelist Zelda Sayre (19) at St. Patrick's Cathedral in New York. Georgia declares independence. (I think it was the country not the state, but I could be mistaken.) Walt Disney started work as an artist with KC Slide

Co for $40 a week. US Post Office says children cannot not be sent by parcel post (after various instances). This is real! I didn't make it up.

By the time I came along, Aunt Ann had married Uncle Clyde, had son and a daughter, and lived in a mansion on the edge of Glen Ellyn. Truthfully, the house wasn't a mansion the way we think of one now, but it was amazing. In a day when many people didn't have indoor plumbing,* (*Our house still had an outhouse attached to the shed in back but we did have indoor plumbing) their house had two (2) indoor bathrooms! I couldn't believe it. They had a basement that didn't have a dirt floor like the cellar at Grandma and Grandpa's farm. They had more than one TV. Unreal! They had a garage big enough to fit two cars, and cars in the 50s were huge. Remember tail fins? I loved when my family would go north in the summer to visit Aunt Ann and Uncle Clyde. I could watch baseball on TV almost every day (even though it was the Cubs.)

Anyway, the world was totally different in 1920. The Spanish flu was the pandemic of choice that year. Oh! Now we have a different pandemic so maybe the world hasn't changed all that much. Aunt Ann might not appreciate the technology we have today, or maybe she does, but I am thankful for the technology that allows me to put this birthday greeting on a platform the whole world can see.

HAPPY BIRTHDAY, AUNT ANN

Thank You, Dr. Whoever You Are

Sorry, those of you who are fans of the British TV series, but this is not about that Dr. Who.

My blogs are often facetious, sometimes sarcastic, hopefully comedic at times and occasionally sincere and heartfelt about the loss of a loved one. This one is different.

Many times we take the skillful people who work in healthcare for granted. It is so common for a doctor to set a broken bone, fill a cavity, crunch your back to make it feel better, insert a pacemaker, transplant a kidney, remove cataracts, replace a broken liver, even give someone a new heart. Modern medicine is a wonder.

Babies are probably born every second of the day, so a new life coming into the world is not seen as something out of the ordinary. We take it for granted that a baby will be born in good health and the mother will nurture her baby until they become responsible adults. (I know it doesn't end with adulthood but go along with me.) Occasionally, this is not the way it happens. Harper, Luna and Gideon, I still think about you.

I was sitting in my comfortable chair in my office last night watching a travel show on YouTube. I got up to get something to munch on or maybe a drink of 7 Up. Doesn't matter. I walked past my wife, who was sitting in her comfortable chair in the living room, and she asked if I had gotten a text from someone. I located my cell phone and stared at it for a few seconds. It didn't come to life, so I assumed I hadn't received a text. She told me what the text was about, and I totally forgot about the 7 Up or the Archway lemon cookies I had in mind. Those of you who know me well will know my eyes are a giveaway to my emotions. (Tough guys should ignore this part and think about fishing, football or souped-up-cars). My eyes have this habit of becoming like a waterfall at times. I retreated to my office and prayed.

I don't text very well, and have sworn off Facebook for the most part, but I decided to use Facebook to message the person who sent my wife the original text. We 'messaged' back and forth, and I offered support (I hope). Eventually, a photo appeared with news of one of God's New Creations. Praise God! All was well. Mom and baby were doing okay. I learned some of the important details... baby's name, weight, etc. I 'messaged' back "She was a big 'un." Over ten pounds! I told my wife the news and she saw the photo. She has lots of hair... The baby not my wife... Well, my wife still has hair, but... never mind.

I thanked God for his blessings. I thanked Him for the doctors who can perform modern miracles likes doing a C-section (Six or seven times in the case of one person I know.) and make it seem routine. No way is it routine for the parents and family involved. In this case the family of four we care deeply about. (5 if Dahlia counts, but she's a dog so she probably doesn't).

So, thank you Dr. Whoever for your amazing work and skill. Maggie is not out of the woods, but God is watching over her.

Random Thoughts of a Strange Mind, Part 3

Yesterday I received the tests results from my recent visit to my doctor. I had been feeling a bit off, so I had made an appointment. He called me personally and said it could be a couple things. He thought it was most likely I was suffering from prosopagnosia exasperated by a mild case of pleurodynia. His other thought was I could have contracted a rare form of emmetropia. His diagnosis sounded rather minascious. I asked him how this happened or where it could have started. He replied the likely source was my abomasum and then asked if I had been having trouble with deglutition. I assured him that was not the case and had not heard any borborygmus, either. He asked if I was taking care of my clepsydra, and I assured him I was following his directions.

I suppressed my cacoethes and refrained from coprolalia. Being an accomplished deipnosophist with hundreds of hours of experience, I decided to take an alternative approach to this tangent. I reminded him of my discobolus. He hemmed and hawed but admitted he had forgotten about that. I jokingly told him to review his course in haruspex.

He suggested I take Benthos daily. If I could find the generic form, Zopissa, that would suffice. I asked if that would interact with my DWAAL, and he assured me the chances were negligible. Since he specialized in posology, I acquiesced to his superior knowledge and assured him I would reduce my emacity accordingly. Considering myself an opsimath in the field, I took his advice with considerable omophagy. At first I considered his suggestion to be rather mumpsimus and asked him about taking Gasconade to avoid dehydration. He replied I could but only if I obnubilate it first.

After following his advice for a week my H-W-Y-L had improved vastly. I talked to him again and he said my results were absolutely incunabula. I decided to celebrate and order an extra large pogey for lunch with adscititious flews. My wife is disgusted by this, but pogeys have been a staple of my diet from childhood.

Some of my relatives add extra fipple to make it crunchier.

After answering the door and turning away a colporteur, I resumed working on my blog with the enthusiasm of a croze. The words flowed mellifluously and I was able to complete the article in only a chiliad. Granted time can be very fugacious, but I try to keep to a schedule and stay away from the local howff. After backing up all my folders to a new bawbee, I unwrapped a chocolate Bezoar and enjoyed a break.

Though I'm not often impressed by the concinnity of my blogs. I felt a great deal of shallop after accomplishing my goal of rubricating the manuscript. I printed it and tossed it in the sternutator for safekeeping.

Thankfully this is a story with a eucatastrophe. I just wish I could remember where I placed my brand new dariole. Perhaps the stylite had moved it deasilly.

You Wanna Buy a New Car, Kid?

"I have the perfect car for you. It won't cost more than both arms and legs, and I will make a huge commission."

I've heard that many times over the years when I first started buying cars. Now, the Internet has all the info you need to get a decent price on a car. I like new cars. I can't remember how many I've purchased over the years. Some we only kept for a year before trading it in on a new one. Only twice have we kept a car long enough to reach 100,000 miles. A 1998 Dodge Grand Caravan and 2006 Honda Accord. Back in the 70s, cars were cheap, and I bought several cheap cars. Does anyone remember the Chevy Vega? I had two. One nice thing about them (maybe the only nice thing) was I could fit my drum kit in the back. Since I often left work and would head to a gig, that was convenient. If only minivans had been available.

We owned three Camaros in the 70s. A '75, '79, and an '81. The '75 drank gas like a person finding an oasis after being in the desert for a week. The '79 was a beautiful car. Navy blue exterior with a baby blue interior. It was totaled before I made the first payment. Unfortunately, the '81 was a dog. A six cylinder with the get up and go of an out of tune Yugo. Most cars of that era were not worth owning. I don't blame GM. It was the government regulations.

I would occasionally buy a used sports car just for fun. I owned a red '79 Fiat X1/9. The X1/9 had a targa top and was a blast to drive, though bicycles would often pass me. I barely fit in the car, but I took it on a road trip to Florida. It handled as if it was on rails, but the lawn mower engine was not very powerful. I sold it and bought a red Mazda RX7. I believe it was a '79, also. It had better pickup, but didn't handle as well as the Fiat. At least I had more room in it. The thing I remember most was having to tune it up every other day.

One of the cars I liked best was a white Plymouth Laser. It was either a 1990 or '91. I can't remember, but it doesn't matter. It was a hatchback, and I could fit my bicycle in the back. By this time I was into bicycle racing and used the car to transport my bike around the Midwest. My son had the car when he went into the navy. When he was overseas, I used the car. Though it was a 'sports' car, it was comfortable on long trips. I drove it to and from Norfolk, Virginia, many times. Eventually, it needed more work than it was worth, so it went to the scrap heap.

I leased an Acura RSX Type S in the early 2000s. That car was a blast. It had a six-speed with a 200 horsepower Honda VTEC engine. It was quick but also got great gas mileage. I would have bought the car after the lease matured, but it didn't have a center console. Now I wish I had bought it.

Every once in a while I get the bug to buy another sports car. I would love a Mazda Miata or a Subaru BRZ or a Porsche Boxter, but getting in and out of a car that low to the ground at my age would get old. If I lived in Florida, Arizona or Southern California. I would buy something sporty like a convertible.

Now my wife drives a Honda CR-V like millions of other people, and I drive a Hyundai Elantra Sport. My little Elantra can get around pretty quick if I press down with my right foot. It's a sleeper car. It's three years old and hasn't reached 20,000 miles yet. Someone will get a good car when I decide to trade it for something new.

FAQs – The Top Ten (or eleven, whatever)

On my website I an often asked the same questions over and over. This is a compilation of the most frequently asked.

Why is there not a photo of you in any of your books?

Vanity. Contrary to popular belief, I do not look like the man sitting in a chair with a cat on his lap that adorns my website. I found that in Shutterbox and decided to use the image since it was free. If you must know, I look exactly like the man at the top of this blog. (On my best days)

Where do you write your intriguing stories?

I have an office in my home. My desk looks out over the front yard enabling me to watch birds frolicking in the iron birdbath just outside my window.

Where do you get the inspiration for your stories?

Years ago I was searching the Metropolis Public Library for a book about the fall of the Habsburg Empire in order to do a research paper for college. I found the correct section and pulled out three dusty books which easily weighed ten pounds apiece. I blew off the dust, coughed for several minutes and then noticed a small paperback wedged behind the tomes. Curiosity took over and I pulled out the small, thin paperback. It was titled *101 Themes to use When writing fiction Guaranteed to Make your Book a best-seller.* Needless to say, I was enthralled especially after noting it was self-published in 1748 by William Godwin. Looking around, I pocketed the slim book and walked out. (I have since returned the book when the library had an amnesty day) Most of the themes of my stories come from this volume. Thank you, Mr. Godwin.

Why do you write?

Perhaps the most often asked question. Especially in person. My answer is simple. I write to confound Spellcheck.

Really, why do you write?

Okay, to be honest. The venerated Greek philosopher of ancient long ago antiquity, Ptolemy Jacobsen, wrote (actually he carved these words into a column of the Acropolis) It is far better for a blind man to rush haphazardly into the dense forest of his mind and confront the white bear face to face than to step on the head of the serpent on the third level of an inner city parking deck. Nuff said.

What is the most tedious part of writing in your opinion?

The endless rewriting; and editing: by far. I attempt to thorougly elinimate any and all mitsakes from my printed manuscripts,

Who are the top five influences in your writing?

First and foremost − Carl Ramos for his use of the word 'greenish' in each of his 47 novels depicting life on the frozen tundra of New South Liechtenstein. Second - Clair Bee − for creating a totally realistic fictional world of sports for junior high boys living in the hills and valleys of rural Pennsylvania. Third - I've always admired the romanticism of Calvin Coolidge's State-of-the-Union addresses. Fourth - I've patterned my style of writing after J. B. Patterson and the late Clyde Cussler who made millions using the same plot for the hundreds of books they publish every year. Lastly, I admire Lee Harper for his nearly unsustainable level of productivity over a 55 year career as a novelist. In a less serious aside, I am fascinated by Erich Schullerstein's use of the word Cattywhampus on every tenth page of his novel depicting life in the hills and dales of medieval Arkansas in the early fifteenth century. (He also spells the word diferntly each time.)

Are you related to the Pleasant H. Johnson who lived in the 300 block of W. Fourteenth Street in Belleville, South Dakota back in the late 60s?

I'm not sure why, but this question pops up roughly once a week and always by different people. As far as I know, I'm not related to Pleasant H. Johnson.

76

What advice can you give to aspiring authors?

I once asked the famous Belgian cyclist, Eddy Merckx, whose victories number more than the grains of rice in a box of Uncle Ben's Brown Basmati, what I should do to become a better cyclist. He responded – Ride, Ride, Ride! I have patterned my response to this inquiry thusly – write, Wright, right, Rite. (And always avoid alliteration)

Are your stories based on real life, or are they total figments of your imagination?

Yes... obviously.

Do you listen to music as you write, and if so – Who is your favorite artist?

If I listen to music while I work it is usually nineteenth century Ecuadorian classical. My favorite composer is Brittany von Spears.

If Harry Potter© and Anne of Green Gables had a love child, would it have red hair and green eyes?

Again, a seemingly random question that pops up from time to time. Not being a geneticist, I would assume this is possible, but the offspring might also have two heads because of the father's involvement with Witchcraft and Sorcery.

When will the Emmy Story end?

Several years ago I wrote Emmy's obituary. She passed away in 2076 at the age of 96. Public outcry was so overwhelmingly negative that I did a Sir Adrian Conan Doyle. In the next book, I allowed one of Emmy's great-granddaughters, who did research in the field of Internal Nanomicrosymbioticgestative Biology in third grade, to miraculously resurrect her. Emmy went on to live another 30 years working as a clerk in the combination general store/HRH post office in the small English village of Machynlleth-on-Senghenwydd, near the border of Wales, experiencing many adventures selling stamps and packets of biscuits to the local shepherds.

Who is your favorite character in the Emmy Books?

Easy! On page 63 of the third book in the series near the bottom is an unnamed character waiting in line at the Sainsbury's. His face is expressionless, he doesn't speak and he stands absolutely still as he waits in the 15-items-or-less aisle fully knowing he has seventeen cans of albacore tuna-in-water in his cart. To me this beguiling person distills the total essence of the Emmy Series. (Don't bother looking for this character because the fourteenth editor of that book cut him out.)

I hope my answers have given you a sense of how I approach the characters and locations I have created for the series of books I lovingly call – *Emmy's Story.*

Withdrawal Pains

This can't be March because there's no Madness! Wait. I take that back. There is madness just not the right kind. The March Madness I'm missing is basketball. College and high school. I don't care about the NBA anymore, but one of the things I look forward to each year are the tournaments. I've only missed a couple of Final Fours (on TV) since I watched Cincinnati beat Ohio State back in '61 or '62. They played in the finals both years and I can't remember which one I saw (or if I saw both of them) I do remember watching Chicago Loyola beating Cincinnati in '63. I guess I'm getting old.

For the first time in over a 110 years there will not be champions in boys basketball in Illinois. The girls were lucky enough to finish in time. What a shame.

To help get over the pain of not hearing One Shining Moment and watching the nets being cut, I decided to hold my own tournament. I printed a blank bracket and picked 64 teams. Sorry about not including the other four teams that have to play the early games. To make this brief, I'll give you the highlights of how the tournament went. First the two top seeds in each region-

East –	1-Florida State	2-Maryland
Mideast* -	1- Dayton	2-Duke
Midwest -	1-Kansas	2- Baylor
West -	1-Gonzaga	2- San Diego State

Biggest upsets and highlights -

Ten Big Ten teams made the tournament and all ten won their opening round games.

Unfortunately for the Duke Blue Devils they had to face Stephen F. Austin again and lost by fifteen points in the first round. Who else saw this coming?

Also in the Mideast region, Illinois took out Dayton and made it to the elite eight.

Experience showed in the Midwest as Michigan State upset Baylor by 12 points.

Kansas reached the Midwest final easily. Their average margin of victory was 29.6 points/game.

In the West Wisconsin defeated San Diego State and faced Gonzaga in the final.

Florida State and Maryland cruised to their match up in the East finals.

Kentucky missed only four free throws in total in reaching the elite eight.

Regional Finals Highlights

East – Maryland defeated Florida State in overtime 57-54

Mideast – Kentucky ended Illinois' magical run with a ten point victory 78-68

Midwest – Kansas defeated Michigan State 72-65. Tom Izzo followed Mark Dantonio's path and retired after the game.

West – no one bothered attending this game but it was later learned that Gonzaga defeated Wisconsin 69-63 to advance to the Final Four.

Final Four Results

In the first game Kentucky prevailed over Maryland mostly because they made 50% of their three-point-shots and 26 out of 29 free throws. Kentucky 86 Maryland 77

In the second game Kansas continued their domination and defeated Gonzaga by 28. No one from Spokane watched on TV. Gonzaga coach Mark Few left immediately after the game for Eastern Europe to find the tallest players he could sign for next year.

Few people gave the young Kentucky team a chance in the final, but when Nick Richard blocked Devon Dotson's shot with one second to go, the Wildcats held on to win by two 69-67. John Calipari and Bill Self shook hands and vowed to return in 2020-

2021 with all new players.

So there you have it. Even if the NCAA didn't crown a champion, I did. If I have to be perfectly honest, I think Kansas would have won it all, but I've been a Kentucky fan since 1966.

P.S. - In other news Olivet Nazarene University won the NAIA II tournament in Sioux Falls, SD, defeating Indiana Wesleyan 96-78. Olivet fans were jubilant even though the Tigers didn't score 100 points.

* it's my tournament so I can name the four regions whatever I want.

Is This Really Emmy?

I have been been going through the early 'Emmy' books doing a bit of fine tuning, and in some cases expanding on the story. I finished the first three books and started on book four. I read through the first chapter and thought it encapsulated Emmy almost exactly as I see her in my mind. I will post it here and on the website. Any comments or questions are appreciated and will be answered in a timely manner. Timely as defined by the Greater Delaware Procrastination Society.

Chapter One

Heavy wet snow continued to fall as Emmy Colasanti crawled along with the other drivers in the early Monday morning traffic. She scanned the FM stations while on her ten mile commute from South Hampshire to Melrose Grove and her job at Robertson Industries. *This music sucks. Doesn't any station play decent music anymore?* She sat at a red light and reached over to the glovebox. She pulled out the Fridays At Five CD *Hero For Hire* and slid it into the recently installed CD player.

Suddenly, the driver in the car behind her leaned on his horn.

"What?" Emmy looked in the rearview mirror.

The driver blasted his horn again.

Emmy looked up at the green light. "Sorry." She waved at the car behind her and raced through the light at a snail's pace as the wheels struggled for traction.

"In a boy's mind as the lights go out." She sang along as the title track played. "Gonna fight fire. Gonna save the girl. I'm a hero for hire."

Despite the heavy traffic on her commute to work, Emmy had reasons to smile. Her boyfriend, Kenny Colwell, had just returned home from California where he and his partners in the band, Fridays At Five, had been recording their new project for the last month. She would see him this evening after work. Not only that, but she and her former boyfriend, Tony Bertucci, mended their broken friendship. He and her best friend, Kristen Keasling, even went to church with her the previous morning in South Bend. She offered a prayer of thanks as she drove into work. She slammed on her brakes as the car in front of her stopped suddenly, yet again.

"I hate this blasted traffic." She pounded on the steering wheel and cringed as her horn blared. *It's days like this that make me wish I could work from home.* Finally, traffic eased, and Emmy made it to work five minutes early. She parked the car and glanced up at the top of the fifteen-story glass and steel building as she walked to the entrance. *I wonder if we'll really get six inches of snow today.* She dashed into one of the elevators just before the door closed.

Mr. Oliver, her office supervisor, had just hung up his coat when Emmy skipped into the office suite. He ran a hand through his thinning, gray hair and grinned as he listened to her singing a song.

"Emmy, you sound so happy today, especially for a Monday. Care to tell me why?"

"Oh, Mr. Oliver, everything is absolutely wonderful today." Her blue eyes sparkled as she took off her coat and tossed it at the coat rack next to her desk.

Mr. Oliver shook his head. "How do you always manage to get your coat to stay on the hook?"

She shrugged and said, "It's all in the wrist. Anyway, Kenny got home late last night. I haven't seen him yet, but I will after work today." She smiled at Mr. Oliver, sighed and said, "I've missed him so much. Oh, and Tony was in a car accident Friday and had to go to the hospital. Isn't life wonderful?"

Mr. Oliver tilted his head and arched his bushy eyebrows. "You're happy that Tony is in the hospital?"

"What?" She landed back in reality with a thud. "Oh, that's not the reason I am so happy. Well, it is in a way. Kenny came home. Not because of the accident, but because of what happened after. He was flying home to see me and got hit by a truck when he was going shopping. The truck totaled his car because of the ice, but the band is home for now."

83

Emmy waved her hands around, talked too fast and didn't make any sense whatsoever.

"Slow down, Emmy. Come and have a seat in my office, and you can tell me all about your weekend."

Emmy followed Mr. Oliver into his floor-to-ceiling glass office and sat facing him.

"Now take a deep breath and tell me what happened, please."

"Okay, it all started Friday night. I wanted to see this band, The Notable Exceptions, because they are one of Kenny's favorites. I've seen them before, and I know P.J. He's the lead singer, and he plays guitar, too. Anyway, Richard wanted to take me to dinner, but I didn't want to go, so he came to the club with me." She still talked a mile-a-minute and waved her hands around and confused Mr. Oliver as much as ever. "I listened to the band. Oh, I saw my friends, Barry and Linda, so we shared their table, and I danced with Barry because Linda's feet hurt. Richard ordered the food. He was drinking beer, but that's besides the point. He took me home…"

Mr. Oliver tilted his head and still looked confused.

"Richard took me home, not Barry and Linda. I made some coffee while he picked out a movie. I sat on the couch with him, but I don't even remember what movie. Oh, I don't know if I should tell you this part."

"You know that anything you tell me in confidence stays right here, Emily." He reached across the desk, grabbed her hands, and held them still. "Now finish your story."

She looked down at their hands. She tried to move her hands, but Mr. Oliver held onto them tightly. "Yes, sir. Okay, I'll tell you." She talked slower now. "Richard and I were watching a movie, and he kissed me and sorta made a pass at me. He became pretty aggressive, and I tried to get away. All of a sudden the phone rang, and it was Mama, Tony's mother. Everyone calls her Mama."

"So I've heard." He let go of her hands.

She immediately began talking faster and waving her hands around. "She left a message that Tony had been in a wreck and an ambulance took him to the hospital. I threw Richard out, and told him I never wanted to see him again and not to ever call me again. I should have listened to Kristen because she warned me about him. I never wanted to be anything more than his friend, but I guess he wanted more." She blushed as she got embarrassed. "Then I called Mama. She told me what she knew, and then I called Kristen. Saturday morning I emailed Kenny to let him know what happened, and we drove to South Bend to see Tony. Not me and Kenny, because he was still in LA at the time, but I took Kristen and Mama to South Bend."

Mr. Oliver rubbed his forehead as he tried to make sense of Emmy's story.

"He's banged up, but he'll be all right. Kristen met John, who is Tony's roommate, at the hospital, and they are gonna fall in love, I just know it. She thinks he's a hunk." Emmy took a breath, sighed and said, "And that is why I am so happy today."

"I'm very happy for you, Emmy." He was still a bit confused, but Emmy smiled with joy, and that thrilled him.

"Thank you, Mr. Oliver."

Everyone in the office soon knew of Emmy's adventurous weekend.

The hours flew by. She locked up all the files and checked her desk. She tossed several letters in the outbox and looked at the clock. "Wow, it's after five already. I wish all days went by this fast."

She knocked on Mr. Oliver's door and entered. "I'm going to take off now unless you need anything else."

"Go ahead. I will be leaving in a few minutes myself."

"Good night, Mr. Oliver."

"Good night, Emmy. See you tomorrow."

Emmy noticed a car parked in the street as she pulled into her driveway. She saw Richard Demarco waiting on the front sidewalk and grimaced as she thought, *Why are you here? I told you to stay away.* Emmy was determined not to have a confrontation with him. She didn't want anything to spoil her relationship with Kenny Colwell, or her renewed friendship with Tony Bertucci. She slammed on the brakes of the red 1993 Honda Civic, threw the transmission into park and opened the door.

She kept her voice calm and under control as she stomped toward him. "What are you doing here, Richard?"

"Hi, Emmy, I wanted to talk to you for a minute. Can I come in?"

"Not a chance! Why are you even here? Did you not understand what I told you on Friday?"

"Emmy, I promise I won't try to kiss you, or even touch you." He held up a hand.

"I know you won't because I won't let you come near me. You can't come in the house."

"Can I talk to you at least?" he pleaded.

"All right, but just for a minute. I'm expecting someone."

Richard didn't move closer as she walked up the front steps. He remained on the front sidewalk with his hands in the pockets of his black trench coat and a fedora covering his graying hair. "Have you gotten back together with Tony? Is he all right?"

"He's going to be fine, and we are friends again, not that it's any of your business." Emmy looked to her right as an icicle fell from the roof gutter and shattered on the frozen ground.

"I suppose that means we are just going to be friends then."

"Hmmmph! I doubt it. I could be a friend, but you showed me that you're not interested in being my friend. You just want to get me in bed, and I can guarantee that ain't gonna happen. Not in this universe. I'm sorry, but that's the way it has to be."

"Is there anything I can do to regain your trust? I'd really like to be your friend. I have enough enemies already," he joked.

"You could move back to Kansas," Emmy said with a straight face. *I'm not falling for your charm again.*

"I do have a few friends who are women."

I find that hard to believe. She rolled her eyes. "If I thought for one second you could keep our relationship platonic, maybe we could still see each other for lunch at work occasionally. But friends? No way in hell are we ever going to be friends."

"Okay, I thought I would make sure you were all right."

"I'm doing great. Goodbye, Richard. Have a nice life," Emmy said sternly as she walked into the house. She watched from inside the front door as Richard walked toward his car. She grinned as he slipped on the snow and landed on his butt. *Shoot! Are you hurt?* She opened the door, but before she stepped outside, Richard rose to his feet, brushed off the snow and with head held high, marched to his car, got in and drove away. *I'm sorry for laughing at you, but that did look funny.*

She felt an icy blast of air as she closed the door. *I hope we don't get all that snow. At least not before Kenny gets home.* She sprinted up the stairs two at a time to her bedroom, ripped off her skirt and top and sat on the bed and struggled to shed her pantyhose. *I wish I never had to wear these things. I hate them with a passion.* She found woolen socks, put on a pair of jeans and a sweatshirt. She was coming down the stairs when she heard the back door open. She stopped to listen and heard footsteps.

"Emmy! Where are you? I let myself in."

"Be right there!" She flew down the stairs, slid around the corner on the hardwood floor and darted into the kitchen where Kenny Colwell met her. She held out her arms and he picked her up and hugged her.

"Hey, Emmy, how are you? How was your weekend? Is Tony okay? Sit on the counter, and tell me everything."

He helped her jump up on the counter.

"Oh, Kenny, I'm so glad you're home. I missed you so much!" She kissed him all over his face. "I'm going to kiss you all night long."

"I missed you, too." He kissed her and ran a hand through her curly dark hair. "You got it trimmed."

"Do you like it? Is it too short?"

"It's still pretty long. It's way past your shoulders."

"I have to tell you what happened…" She began to tell him about the weekend as fast as she could possibly speak.

"Slow down, Em. Start with the phone call you got from Mama, okay?"

Emmy took a deep breath and calmed down. "I should start with earlier Friday. I went to see The Notable Exceptions with Richard Demarco from work. We ran into Barry and Linda at the club and sat at a table with them. Richard wanted to leave, so he brought me home. I let him come in—big mistake." She waved her hands in the air. "We were sitting on the couch in the TV room, and he tried to kiss me. He actually did kiss me. Against my will." She kept bouncing up and down on the countertop. "The phone rang, and it was Mama. She left a message that Tony had been in an accident and was in the hospital. I told Richard to leave and called Mama."

"Is Tony all right?"

"He broke his arm and has some bruises and scrapes, but he's okay." She paused and wasn't sure what to say next.

"Who is this Richard guy?"

"It's a long story…"

"I've got all the time in the world," Kenny said as he grinned. He put his hands on the counter on either side of her. He leaned forward and kissed her again.

She wrapped her arms around his neck and held on tight. They kissed until they ran out of breath.

"I like that," Kenny said.

"Me, too." She kissed him one more time. "Okay, he's the guy who used to deliver the mail, but he got a job in Kansas and just got back a short time ago. I met him in the elevator, and we ate dinner and lunch."

Kenny laughed as she waved her hands all around.

"He's older and used to be married, but I don't think he is now. Kristen and Barry think he looks old enough to be my father because he has some gray hair. I thought he was nice, but he tried to kiss me, and I told him I never wanted to see him again. He was here when I got home from work today, but I didn't let him in. I told him to go away and never call me or see me again. Kristen was right about him." Emmy paused for breath.

Kenny smiled at Emmy. "Oh, I missed you so much. I could listen to you all night long. You can tell me more about this guy later. I'm glad Tony is all right."

"He'll be fine. Did I mention that we met his roommate? His name is John Randolph, and he likes Kristen. Kristen thinks he's a hunk, and they are in love. They may not know it yet, but they are."

"You are so funny, Em. Didn't Tony try to set you up with

88

him before?"

"Yeah, but I wasn't interested. Now it's a good thing."

Kenny kissed her again, and she responded by kissing him for as long as she could breathe.

"Are you hungry?" Kenny asked. "Should we go somewhere, or eat here?"

"Let's eat here, so I can tell you about everything that has happened since you've been in LA. Did you see Becky at all?"

"Yes, I did. I ate dinner with her and her whole family twice, but we never went out by ourselves."

"It would be okay if you did. I know you're still friends."

"What do you have for dinner?" Kenny opened the fridge. "I see you have the ingredients for a salad. I can make that."

"I bought stuff to make Reuben sandwiches. Do you like those?"

"Yeah, I do. Do you have real corned beef or the canned version?"

"I bought the real stuff at the deli. It's almost St. Patrick's Day, so I thought I would fix some Irish food. I bought soda bread and even found a green sweater at Kohl's to wear to work."

"Ah! You need a new jumper with the fierce weather we been havin'." Kenny used his approximation of an Irish accent.

"What?" Emmy squinted her eyes.

"A sweater is called a jumper in Ireland. Ah, never mind."

Such a dork. Emmy shook her head. "You still have a few days to work on being Irish."

They both worked on getting dinner ready and ate in the TV room while watching *Father Of The Bride* on DVD.

"Have you ever seen the original version?" Kenny asked.

She held a finger up as she chewed on her Reuben sandwich. "Yes, but I like this version better. Steve Martin is perfect for this role and the actress playing is daughter is adorable. I love her hair."

"She sorta reminds me of you except your hair is longer."

"Yeah, and I'm better at basketball than her. She dribbles and shoots like a girl."

"Duh!" Kenny held out his hands.

"You know what I mean." Emmy poked him in the side.

While they ate, Emmy told him everything that happened lately.

"It's already eleven." Kenny checked the time later. "I need to run, Em."

She kissed him. "Wouldn't you rather stay here?"

"Yes, but I can't. I'll see you tomorrow."

Emmy grabbed her coat and followed him to his car alongside the house. "It's still snowing. The roads might be treacherous with all this fierce weather we been having. Maybe you should stay."

"Are you making fun of my accent?" Kenny used his arm to clear some snow from the top of his car and flung it at Emmy.

"Hey! Stop that!" She jumped back and then scooped up some snow, pressed it into a snowball and threw it at him.

He ducked. "Missed me!" He laughed just as she launched a second one.

"Got you with that one," she squealed.

Kenny lunged at her and grabbed her coat before she could escape. He put his arms around her and lifted her onto the front fender of his car. He put his hands on her shoulders and rubbed his nose against hers.

Emmy grinned and asked, "Is that an Irish kiss?"

"It's the way Eskimos kiss."

"I'm not an Eskimo." She pressed her lips to his.

"Em, I can't stay," he said after breaking off the kiss.

"Please be careful going home."

She helped him clean off the three inches of snow from his car.

"See you tomorrow," Kenny said.

She waved as he started to back out of the drive. Then she reached down, formed a large snowball and threw it at his car.

He ducked as the snowball hit the windshield.

Emmy laughed. *You are a dork, but I still love you. Even if you have funny ears.*

Would You Like a Stick of Gum?

For many years this was a question heard by the children at Crystal Lawns Church of the Nazarene. The lady passing out the gum was known by several names. Some children (and a few adults who shall remain anonymous, like Gina) called her Grandma. Others, who were more formal, called her Mrs. Smith. I called her Mrs. Smith for years just to tease her, but most people called her Auntie Doris. She always referred to me as 'her son' and she was like a second mom to me. Sheila and I lived in the apartment over their garage when we were a lot younger.

Ron and Doris Smith were charter members of our church, and I can remember Doris introducing me to Gary and Tim. Our families became good friends and would often picnic together. The Smiths opened their home to the youth group from church. Those were the 'dates' I would take Sheila on. To share a secret, I was sitting in my car in their driveway with Sheila after one of those youth group meeting and said those three magic words. Yep! That's where I first said 'I love you.' She probably doesn't remember it. FYI this was before we were married and living above the garage.

Ron passed away many years ago, and this past week Doris...
Well, you get the picture. I wish there was a way to show you how difficult it was to find the words to write, and I will never admit to getting choked up while attempting to put some meaningful words on paper. (I mean the computer.).

A couple of weeks ago I was on the platform playing the drums with the worship team and glanced out at the congregation. My eyes wandered to the place were Doris always sat. There was an empty space in the pew. I almost lost it because I knew I would never see her sitting there again. I managed to keep the beat and no one saw the tears in my eyes.

In my Emmy Series, I use my church as the basis for the fictional Crest Ridge United Nazarene Church. I have changed the names of the characters who attend to protect their privacy. Though it's pretty easy to tell who some of them are. I didn't change the name of two characters. Ron and Doris Smith. I've also used the garage apartment where Sheila and I lived as a setting in the early books. My Emmy character lived there for a time. Below are some of the scenes from the Emmy books that include Aunt Doris.

"Your husband?" Emmy turned to Paul and smiled. "You didn't tell me Lynette was your wife."

"I am sorry for that bit of deception, but I wanted to surprise both of you. Please forgive me." He grinned like a Cheshire cat. "Lynette, do you want me to see if Aunt Doris can step in and take over the class for you? I think Emmy would like to talk to you privately."

"Thanks, Paul."

Lynette and Emmy talked for a moment as they waited for Aunt Doris to take over the class. Aunt Doris entered and took over without missing a beat. Lynette and Emmy found a place to talk privately.

"Why don't you come with me to my class, and you can help me with the kids?"

Emmy followed Lynette back to the classroom full of children.

"Aunt Doris, this is my friend Emmy. She is a new believer."

"Hello, Emmy, I'm not really her aunt, but everyone around here calls me Aunt Doris. You can call me that, too, if you want. Would you like a piece of gum, dear?"

Emmy shyly smiled and nodded her head.

As Emmy and Kenny headed toward an exit, he saw Mr. Cartwright and his wife again. He wondered what he must think as he saw him with Emmy. He didn't have a chance to talk to him though as some of the teenagers surrounded him. He took time to talk to them and felt embarrassed as he signed a few autographs. Most of the crowd had left by the time Kenny and Emmy finally were able to get away. They saw Pastor Ausland as he talked to the church treasurer, Ron Smith, and his wife, who Emmy knew as Aunt Doris.

"Who is that?" Christopher asked Emmy.

"Mr. Smith. He's the church treasurer. He and Aunt Doris have been members since the very beginning."

"Aunt Doris?" Christopher looked puzzled as he tilted his head.

"I'll explain later."

Doris Smith rose to her feet. "I would like to say something if I may."

Tyler nodded. "You may."

"Ron and I have been members of this church from the beginning..." She began.

Liz grabbed her wireless mic and hurried down the steps and over to the spot where Ron and Doris always sat.

"You should use this, Auntie Dorie, so everyone can hear you." Liz handed Doris the mic.

"I don't know how to use this, honey." She looked at the microphone as if it were alive and might attack her.

Liz grinned and said, "You hold it up and talk into it. It won't bite you."

"Thank you, sweetie." Doris tried to remember where she left off but couldn't, so she started again.

Doris stopped and one of the other ladies stood up.

It's been a habit of mine to close up the church after Sunday's service. Invariably, there would be a few people socializing well after church had ended. I would wait patiently until they finished, but every once in a while I would nudge them along. I would say "Church is over now, Doris. It's time to go home." She would laugh at me and tell me to behave.

93

Today as Pastor Tyler and I were getting ready to leave, I thought about what I would say to Doris. I was tempted to utter those words again, but I didn't want Pastor Tyler to think I was goofy. Well, any goofier than I am.

I'm not sure what it's like in heaven, but I do know this.

Doris, you can stay for all eternity. No one is going to tell you to leave. Oh, and I would like a piece of Juicy Fruit when I get there.

This Post Is Meaningless

As my head of PR and I were driving to an event the other day, he mentioned I had not added a post to the website in several weeks. I explained the reason why. Laziness and trying to get through the entire *Downton Abbey* series on Amazon Prime. I love a campy comedy. He told me to get back to work and earn him some money. When I returned home, I dug my trusty Smith-Corona Speedline out of its case, inserted a piece of paper, adjusted the ribbon and began typing.

Hkfk eto iupm bndbg fikt ujkb jgkjherj hjzp fpvjge supe rcali fra gylistic fjklg rlep snfl.

I paused to read what I had written. Then I remembered to turn on the Spelchek.

For hours I sat at my desk gazing out the window and chuckling at the birds trying to take a bath in the solid block of ice in my rusty, iron birdbath. Nothing useful appeared on any of the twenty-seven sheets of paper I used. I rang for the under-butler to clear the mess in my office.

I decided to resort to what recording artists sometimes do to fulfill their contract. A greatest hits album. Though in my case it will be a list of the titles of blogs that didn't make it to the website for one reason or other. Here they are in no meaningful order.

"Famous Actors Who Should Have Changed Their Names But Didn't"

"What Came First? O Henry the Candy Bar or O Henry the Writer?"

"The Complete Log of the 1879 Scientific Expedition of the Yacht *The Gilded Age* to the Foothills of the Himalayas, Part 1"

95

"Stephen King Used a Ghost Writer, and I have the Proof"

"212 Simple Ways to Use Dijon Mustard To Clean Your Home"

"Uncovered! The Secret Life of Albert Einstein as a Barber"

"Why Does Meaningless Need Two 'S's, But Meaningful Is Only Allowed One 'L'?"

That post was followed up with "Who Inv'ented Punc/tuation and, Why?"

"Hidden Messages in Corporate Logos. Can You Spot Them?"

One from the Greater Delaware Procrastination Society "The Merits of Calvin Coolidge's Reticence and Its Effect on Today's Holiday Season"

The list could go on and on, but those were the best of the lot. I have not been completely apathetic toward writing the last two months. I did write another Rex Ford & Clay Horn story. I just need to finish the last chapter. The last chapter always introduces the next installment, and I haven't come up with the plot for the next adventure. Maybe Rex and Clay could visit England and go undercover as a valet and footman for Lord Bonneville.

From the Orpheus Choir to Kinmundy

Sunday evening I decided to forgo watching the NCAA basketball tournament to attend a performance by the Orpheus Choir of Olivet Nazarene University. I am a huge college basketball fan so this was a major sacrifice on my part. Duke University would be playing at the same time as the concert, and I love to root against them for the same reason I cheer for any team playing Tom Brady and the Patriots. I hadn't heard the Orpheus Choir in many years and realized the chance any of the students I had heard before still being in college twenty-five years later would be rather slim. I picked up my son and grandson and met at the church to carpool to Chicago Heights. Eight of us crammed into Tyler's minivan and being the oldest by several decades, I grabbed the front passenger seat.

We arrived at the Chicago Heights Church of the Nazarene early enough to have our choice of seats. I took a program from one of the friendly ushers and entered the sanctuary down the middle aisle. Since no one wanted to choose where to sit, I picked an empty row and we claimed it for our own. I sat in the next-to-last seat by the side aisle with my grandson, Ben, next to me. Pastor Randy welcomed everyone and prayed for the service. Then the choir made their entrance. They used the side aisles and surrounded everyone. Ben was thrilled to see them in their fancy robes. I knew he was excited because he was grinning from ear-to-ear. (Sorry for the cliché, Denise, but this is just a blog.) There were choir members standing right next to us. I could have thrown Phoebe's baby doll and hit them with ease, but I didn't want to upset Phoebe. I noticed that college kids are a lot younger-looking than when I was their age. I glanced around the sanctuary and tried to count how many singers there were. I counted up to ten and then had Phoebe help me. She counted to seventy and then stopped. She is almost two now and a whole lot smarter than me. Anyway, the choir began to sing and I noticed the young lady standing at the end of our aisle. To use another cliché, she looked as pretty as a picture and had the voice of an angel. I hope she, or any of her friends, never read this because she will be embarrassed and her friends will use it to blackmail her or something. After singing a couple songs, the choir took their places on the platform. Somewhere along the way I perused the program and found a section listing the members of the choir, their hometowns and majors. I happened upon one name and was surprised to read she was from Salem, Il. I found that interesting because I was born in that town many hundreds of years ago. I thought it might be interesting to meet her and ask her if she had ever heard of Kinmundy.

I should explain that I would not have even been at the concert except I felt the Holy Spirit urging me to pass up the basketball games.

Later at the end of the program, the choir returned to their positions along the walls of the sanctuary. I again noticed the same young lady standing a few feet away. I looked at the doll in my hands and resisted the urge to throw it at her. The choir sang their last song and exited. Tyler asked if we wanted to stay for the refreshments or head back home. Since there were cookies, Ben wanted to stay. Actually, I wanted to grab a couple cookies too because I hadn't eaten anything for dinner. We headed to the gym and I decided to be brave and ask one of the choir members if they new the young lady from Salem. To protect her privacy, I will refer to her as... uh... how about... I'll call her 'Ashtyn.' That's a pretty name and no one will ever guess her real name. The first person I asked did not know her. I figured it wasn't meant to be. I helped Phoebe eat her cookie and spotted two ladies who looked young enough to be first graders and asked if they were members of the choir. They said they were. Again, I asked if they knew... what name was I using? Oh, right. 'Ashtyn.' I overcame my natural shyness and asked if they knew her. They did! I asked if she was there tonight and they looked around the gym and pointed her out. I thanked them and decided to be brave and approach 'Ashtyn.' I took Ben along because he will talk to anyone. He's six remember. I walked over to the round table on the far side of the gym and three of the students looked at me. I thought about running away, but my feet were stuck in cement and I couldn't move. I managed

98

to summon up the courage to explain my presence.

"I'm looking for... 'Ashtyn,'" I said softly hoping not to be laughed at.

One of the young ladies turned around and said, "I'm... that person whose identity I am protecting."

You have probably already guessed that it was the same young lady with the voice of an angel who was standing only a few feet away before. I was blown away. I asked her if she was indeed from Salem and when she answered in the affirmative, I blurted out that I was born in the Salem Hospital. I was even more surprised to learn that she indeed knew of Kinmundy. There are only a handful of people in the whole world who have ever heard of my hometown and the chances of ever running into one of them is larger than the odds of winning a large fortune playing the lottery. Twice. We talked for a moment and she asked me if I knew someone. I'll call him... uh... I need a good name to protect his privacy... how about... Okay, I'll use the name 'Denzel.' She asked if I knew this person, and lo and behold (Okay, last cliché for this blog) Not only did I know this person, but we were in the same class in school! What a small world.

Then she surprised me even more by saying, "He's my grandfather."

After fixing my jaw and regaining the use of my voice, I managed to say something totally stupid but she was kind enough to pretend I had some degree of intelligence. Having Ben and Kevin with me saved the day. And to think none of this would have happened if I hadn't listened to the Holy Spirit telling me to skip the basketball games and go to hear the Orpheus Choir.

When I got home and checked the scores, I learned that UCF almost took out Duke with a last second shot. I wonder if the result would have been any different had I been watching the game on TV.

The Dallas Cowboys Win the Superbowl!

No, I don't mean this year even though they might win their division with a losing record, but what if next year the NFC East is even worse. Consider this. All the teams in the division are terrible now and probably won't get any better next year. It's highly unlikely but actually possible that each team (Dallas, Philadelphia, Washington, New York) finishes the 2020 season with a losing record. It's possible for each of them to lose every game they play outside of the division. In a sixteen-game season, division teams play only six games against each other. Suppose all four teams lose every game except when they play each other. I'm discounting ties in this crazy scenario because they are so rare these days. What if all four teams split their division games? They all finish with 3-13 records. One of them has to win the division and the NFL has a list.

Three or More Clubs

(Note: If two clubs remain tied after third or other clubs are eliminated during any step, tie breaker reverts to step 1 of the two-club format).

1. Head-to-head (best won-lost-tied percentage in games among the clubs).
2. Best won-lost-tied percentage in games played within the division.
3. Best won-lost-tied percentage in common games.
4. Best won-lost-tied percentage in games played within the conference.
5. Strength of victory.
6. Strength of schedule.
7. Best combined ranking among conference teams in points scored and points allowed.
8. Best combined ranking among all teams in points scored and points allowed.
9. Best net points in common games.

10. Best net points in all games.
11. Best net touchdowns in all games.
12. Coin toss

Suppose the Cowboys are declared division winners on a coin toss? They would be the four seed in the playoffs and host the highest seeded wild card team. Right now the San Francisco 49sers are the top wild card team. What if this happens again next year. Let's say Seattle has another outstanding year and wins the division with a 15-1 record. The 49ers could finish 14-2 and be a fifth seed in the playoffs. The Cowboys would host the 49ers.

As anyone who has been a longtime fan of sports knows, the best team doesn't always win. Suppose everything falls into place for the 3-13 Cowboys and the dormant offense suddenly comes to life. The Cowboys could upset the 49ers, play the Seahawks in the next round, win that game by a single point, travel to... let's say... New Orleans for the conference championship and upset the Saints. That would put the Cowboys in the Superbowl with a record of 6-13. Their opponent would of course be Tom Brady and the Patriots. I don't think that's too much of a stretch.

Anything can happen in the Superbowl. Just ask the Atlanta Falcons, the New York Giants or the New England Patriots. Suppose the Superbowl comes down to the last two minutes and Tom Brady is running out the clock with a two-point lead. Odds are the Patriots would win. But what if Brady is trying to escape the pocket, stumbles (he has never been the most graceful QB) and fumbles or throws an interception and the Cowboys get the ball back. Suppose they move into position to try a field goal with only two seconds left in regulation. The fans in the stadium would be going bonkers! The TV cameras would focus on Jerry Jones. Jason Garrett, who had been given one more chance to prove he isn't the worst coach in Cowboys' history, turns to the the replacement kicker who had been signed to replace the injured Cody Parkey. Adam Vinatieri trots onto the field and makes his only field goal of the year to win the Superbowl against the team he first played for thirty some odd years ago (Okay, it was only 27 or 28 years ago but Vinatieri is almost old enough to be on Medicare)

101

This would be the biggest upset in the history of upsets! Bigger than the Cubs winning a World Series. Bigger than Truman beating Dewey!

My question is... would Jerry Jones be satisfied with winning the Superbowl, or would he fire the entire team for finishing with a record of 7-13?

Look, Ma! I'm in the Paper...

… and I didn't do anything wrong.

The small town in southern Illinois where I lived as a youth supported a weekly newspaper. *The Kinmundy Express*. There were only a few reasons to have your picture in the paper. One might be when you got married, but that wasn't a certainty. Another would be when you passed away and that was more likely. I know I haven't passed away because my wife checks the obituaries for me. She promised to tell me if she read mine. Another reason to have your photo in the paper was if you did something wrong like getting arrested. I have never been arrested, so that would not be a reason for my photo to be published.

My mother-in-law was visiting with my wife Saturday and casually mentioned she saw my picture in the *Herald-News* again. I wasn't sure if she meant recently or a while ago. I usually know in advance if I'm going to be in the paper. At church Sunday one of the ladies handed me an article she had cut out from the paper. She knows I don't subscribe and rarely see a printed paper. I thanked her and looked at the article. I saw the photo I use on my website and read the article. I was completely surprised. My friend, Denise Baran-Unland, is going to 'review' one of my books. I was thrilled. She never reviews books without reading them first. This meant she had actually read one of my books. She is one of the busiest people I know, so for her to take the time to read my book means a lot.

I don't know what she will write in her review, but I can't wait to read it. My books are not going to appeal to everyone. I don't write about superheroes or vampires or fantastical creatures. My granddaughter, who is the reason I began writing in the first place, would rather read her Harry Potter books, but that's okay. My stories are about real life even though they are fiction. Even my main characters are 'real people.' Rock stars do get married (many of them multiple times) and miracles do happen even today. My books usually have happy endings (unless they end on a cliffhanger) and situations get resolved. I know I am a better writer

103

today than when my first book came out. (Insert plug for WriteOn Joliet here) I hate reading my first book now.

Thank you, Denise, for sharing your expertise over the years. Without your persuasiveness, I would still be tweaking my manuscripts. It feels good to have a bookcase shelf lined with books with my name on the spine. I appreciate the many times you have found space in the *Herald-News* to squeeze in an article about me (and all the other local authors.) I'm anxiously awaiting what you have to say about Emmy and her friends. Maybe I would interest more readers if I reveal that the 'Kenny' character is actually a vampire from another planet who has magical superpowers and Emmy is an undercover agent for the CIA... Nah! They're just regular people living in a midwestern city trying to raise a family. Hey! Maybe Kevin Michael could be a superhero...

A Basketball Bouncing in the Dirt

Fifty years ago I was starting my senior year of high school when the phone rang. I don't remember the exact time, or who took the call, but I remember the news it brought. Kevin Ambuehl was gone. He was seventeen and had perished in a drowning accident. I was seventeen, too, and could not fully understand the impact this could have on a family. I still don't because I've never experienced it, and I pray I never do.

Kevin was my friend though we didn't often see each. Our family had moved up north in 1963 leaving our little town of Kinmundy. The Ambuehls lived on a farm north of town. I can remember how to get there, but the old farmhouse is gone which means the old barn is gone, too. I remember the basketball hoop on the barn and how we would play on the dirt court.

I remember his sister Janeen, but she was younger and friends with my sisters. I probably teased her if I spoke to her at all in those days. I don't remember much about the funeral service other than it was in the gym at the LaGrove High School (now known as South Central.) All I know for sure is that I was there. I remember going out to the cemetery, but I don't know if I talked to anyone. I wouldn't have known what to say then, and I don't now, either. My parents might have talked to LaVerne and Marcelline, Kevin's parents, because they were friends.

I don't often get to Kinmundy or Farina, and I haven't been to the Farina cemetery since that day. I might have to take a little trip just to visit old memories. Maybe I could drive past the sight of the old farm and pause. If I listen hard enough, maybe I will hear the sound of a basketball bouncing in the dirt.

Janeen, I know you miss your older brother to this day. I miss him, too, and I think of him when I see my Kevin. I don't remember the exact time I decided to name my son after your brother, but God gave me a son and we named him Kevin. Never thought about any other name. So, Kevin LaVerne Ambuehl, if there's an old dirt basketball court in heaven, I want a rematch, and this time I'm gonna win.

105

Honey Baby Turns Forty

Sadly, I'm not talking about my daughter, but the doll she's holding in her arms. My wife figures this photo was taken shortly after my daughter's third birthday. We don't remember the exact date, but it has to be close. If you look into her eyes, you can see how much she loves Honey Baby. If you were to look into my eyes right now, you would see pools of tears yet to fall. Forty years ago my wife and I were in our twenties, living in our own home a few miles away from my parents. We had decent jobs, a house, a huge garage with the average two-and-a-half cars inside and two precious young-uns. (Wow! Spellcheck let me get away with that.) We were living the good life. The American Dream. We even had a dog if memory serves me correctly.

"Hi, Mom. What's up?"
"You better come over because your father doesn't feel well."

Forty years later I obvious don't remember Mom's exact words, but it was something along those lines. I ran out to the garage and jumped into one of the two-and-a-half cars. I can't remember if I broke all the speeding laws or just some of them as I raced home. I do remember that we took Dad to St. Joe's and he never returned.

Six days later the family watched as the numbers on the heart monitor began slowly counting down. Dad was in a coma for five of those days. He was only fifty-five. Mom later said she was thankful for those days because it gave her the much needed time to adjust to his being gone.

What does this have to do with Honey Baby? Mom and Dad had been Christmas shopping earlier that day before he began not to feel well. Honey Baby was the last present he ever bought. Papa loved his two grandchildren. Maybe that's part of why I love mine so much my heart aches. Maybe that's why I love my 'adopted' grandchildren from church. Yes, Phoebe Grace, I mean you and Phineas and Isaiah and Harper and Walter and all the rest of the young-uns at church. Rosey and Gio, where have you been? I miss you, too.

You can't tell by reading this on your computer, or other mobile device I've yet to figure out, but there was a two-and-a-half minute pause between paragraphs. The tears-that-were-yet-to-fall flooded my old, large-type, three-color keyboard. It's okay. I have a spare still in the box in the closet of my office.

This part is just for Dad, but I suppose you can read it if you want. It's 4:30 in the morning and the words are flowing.

I'm sorry for all the pain I might have caused you and I'm thankful for any joy I might have afforded you. I still miss you forty years later, but I have a hope in my heart. That Hope is Jesus Christ. Because of that hope I know we will see each other again someday. None of us know exactly how it all works after we pass from this life, and that's totally fine with me. I have the faith to sustain me.

P.S. My old keyboard seems to have survived the floofjqr9tukjnb iuhg98d6htjqhgkfhfh.............................. …....... ….
… .. .

The Apolitical Blues, Part III

My wife and I decided to share her list of top U.S. Presidents live on national TV. Okay, we were eating pizza in my office while watching reruns of *The Many Loves of Dobie Gillis*. She came up with her list on her own. I didn't try to influence her at all. Here it is.

Favorite Presidents

1. Abraham Lincoln: I feel a connection with him because he named my Mom's grandfather. It was rare in that day for triplets to survive after birth. President Lincoln named him, Simon Cameron, after his Secretary of War. Abraham Lincoln, like me, is from Illinois. I have visited his historic sites throughout Illinois. Abraham Lincoln was a very brave man.

2. George Washington: He has to be at the top of my list. He was there when it all happened. He was tall. I like tall men. He looked good on a horse.

3. Thomas Jefferson: I'm impressed by the man who could speak, read and write in a number of languages. That's quite an accomplishment. He wrote much of the Declaration of Independence and I live its benefits every day. But most of all, Thomas Jefferson is credited as the creator of the swivel chair and I love swivel chairs.

4. Zachary Taylor: He was a descendant of Elder William Brewster, a Pilgrim leader of the Plymouth Colony, a Mayflower immigrant, and a signer of the Mayflower Compact.

5. Andrew Jackson: On January 1, 1835, Jackson paid off the entire national debt, the only time in U.S. history that has been accomplished. I wish more of our presidents were as concerned about our debts.

6. Ulysses Grant: I've been to Galena, Illinois. Its a nice historic town. Also, in March 1872, Grant signed legislation that established our first national park, Yellowstone National Park. I have visited several of our national parks.

7. John Adams: He never owned a slave. This is a good thing. I think I visited his home, too.

8. Rutherford B. Hayes: He believed education was important. He said, "free government cannot long endure if property is largely in a few hands and large masses of people are unable to earn homes, education, and a support in old age." Also, he was a supporter of prison reform.

9. Dwight D. Eisenhower: He was president when I was born. He authorized the Interstate Highway System which I have used a lot to travel around the country.

10. Ronald Reagan: He grew up in Illinois. He was a movie star before he became president which proves that only in America can the unthinkable happen.

These did not make my top 10 list but I am impressed with them. William Henry Harrison because he delivered the longest inaugural address in American history. It took him nearly 2 hours to read it. That requires determination. James Buchanan because he kept an elephant at the White House. I'm surprised they let him do that. Theodore Roosevelt because he spent 90 minutes giving a speech after he had been shot. That shows stamina.

I read her list, and though I agree with some choices, I am flabbergasted by her decision to totally ignore our greatest president of all time. Millard Fillmore. I can only assumes she did it as a joke, but then what do I know. I am the most apolitical person she knows.

101 Ways To Prepare Eggplant

I am a huge fan of eggplant. I love eggplants of all different sizes and shapes. The color is perfect and it is one of the most versatile vegetables God has created. A great chef once told me he could prepare eggplant in more ways than there are shades of red. Not only is the eggplant visually appealing, it is full of nutrition. I don't know the exact numbers, but I think eggplant provides 100% of the daily requirements of purple food. The old saying should have been 'an eggplant a day keeps the doctor away.'

My favorite president, Millard Fillmore, ate eggplant every day in the White House. He claimed it helped clear his mind and enabled him to make difficult decisions. Who can argue with that? He tried to enact legislation to have the eggplant declared the national vegetable instead of the potato. Had he succeeded we would be eating purple French fries made of eggplant every time we go through a drive-in window at our local fast-food restaurant.

The most common way to prepare eggplant is of course on the grill. You prepare it much like a t-bone steak. The big difference is eggplants aren't as bloody and they are purple instead of red when eaten rare. They are also boneless which is another plus. Another common way to prepare eggplant is to slice it thinly, fry it in a pan with butter and use it on a sandwich instead of fried bologna. Either one is delicious and nutritious.

Eggplant soup is a great way to warm your insides on a cold winter night while sitting in your favorite chair and reading the latest book by your favorite author. My suggestion would be to read any book by Kenneth Lee McGee. I add bacon and diced rutabaga to my soup though my wife likes to replace the rutabaga with beets or kohlrabi. Any combination works.

Clarence Pastyoureyes genetically created baby eggplant by combining a regular plant with a toy football enabling chefs all over the world to make mini pizzas for the first time. I didn't realize until I started researching the Internet for this article that eggplant is the eighty-third most popular ingredient added to pizzas with a crust thicker than four inches. Amazing!

Eggplant can be fried, boiled, baked, broiled, sauteed, blackened, grilled, steamed, blow-torched, stomped on, used for insulation in igloos among other uses. I can't think of another vegetable so versatile.

One piece of trivia often overlooked happened on November 6, 1869. The first ever college football game. Rutgers played the College of New Jersey (later known as Princeton University) in New Brunswick, New Jersey before a crowd of 127 fans who each paid a penny for the privilege. The first hour of the contest was used to determine whether or not players would be allowed to touch the pigskin with their hands. It was decided by both coaches that players would not be allowed to touch the ball with any part of their body either above or below the ankle. All went well until a local dog darted onto the field, grabbed the pigskin and sprinted away never to be seen again. Though reports on the ten o'clock news later that night reported the dog and several other mongrels had been seen playing soccer on 55th St. in Brooklyn. This report was later retracted after it was discovered the dog had purchased the pigskin in a local deli. Since neither team had another pigskin the game was nearly canceled. Fortunately, the local green grocer was in attendance and offered the use of his oddly shaped eggplant. Though it was not round like the pigskin they were using, the teams decided to give it a try. After the game players praised the eggplant for its unique shape and durability. Thus, the modern shape of the football was established. In the only other game played that year, a second eggplant was used. No dogs were allowed within fifty yards of the gridiron.

Okay, I might have been a little too ambitious in proclaiming there are a 101 ways to prepare eggplant. My wife and I put together a list and though we racked our brains for two or three minutes, we could not come up with more that 96 ways to prepare either regular or baby eggplant. I was going to change the title, but she said she would find five more ways to cook our favorite vegetable.

Coming next week will be my blog about the many different ways kohlrabi can be used to supplement the diet of native people living in the Arctic Circle. You won't want to miss it.

112

Kohlrabi: The Unappreciated Veggie

I continue my series of blogs about vegetables with what I feel is one of the most overlooked and under appreciated vegetables of our time. Since first being brought to the shores of North America by pioneering UPS driver Ansgar Haerviu in 1635, kohlrabi, though nutritious and extremely popular among reindeer herders in the Arctic Circle, remains relatively unknown in southern Texas and among unemployed cowboys living on Staten Island. Haerviu mistakenly loaded his brown wagon full of kohlrabi onto a ship thinking it was bound for Monaco. He was hoping to sell the produce to the casino and make a quick franc. Instead the ship was blown off course by Hurricane Wendy and ended up in what is now New York harbor. After paying an exorbitant tax for importing strange little green vegetables, Haerviu sold the vegetable door-to-door from his brown wagon through the streets of Little Italy where plump little Italian grandmothers bought it and gave it to their husbands to use playing bocce ball.

Kohlrabi might be considered the black sheep of the wild cabbage family. *Brassica oleracea* in technical terms. Thought to have originated in Bamburg, Germany, in or around 1543, kohlrabi was first mentioned out loud by Frau Becker as she gossiped with her sister-in-law, Frau Meyer, about her neighbor's daughter being seen kissing the baker's son in broad daylight. The baker's son, Walter Hauer, later admitted to stealing the kiss.

While digging in her garden earlier that summer, Frau Brittany Becker pulled up a plant she thought was a weed. Since she needed something for dinner, she added the bulbs to her soup. To her surprise, the bulbs of the plant proved to be a delicious addition to the soup she served that night to her family and the strange little man boarding in the spare room under the attic. Though her family survived after experiencing severe cramps and nausea, the strange boarder succumbed. His last words were "'I thought the soup needed more salt, but I loved the...'" He passed away before finishing his thought.

In spite of this rough start, kohlrabi soon thrived in the small German town later to become famous as the home of the original bratburger. As stomachs became adjusted to the woody-tasting bulbs, the medicinal effects of kohlrabi were discovered. Pharmaceutical giant, Pills-R-Us, began packaging the wonder drug under the brand name Alabaslar. Truck farms specializing in different types of kohlrabi sprung up all over the mountains of Germany and the southern section of Liechtenstein. Wherever there was tillable land, kohlrabi plants replaced the more popular hops and barley. Brewers of the era attempted to use kohlrabi to make beer, but except for a few microbreweries, the foul-tasting beverage never caught on and was soon exported solely to reindeer herders in the Arctic village of Milwaukee.

Once UPS started shipping kohlrabi to the New World, the versatile plant became a staple of transplanted Bavarians living in the neighborhoods of Cleveland, Ohio. The greater Cleveland area became the largest grower of kohlrabi in North America thanks to the efforts of Frau Beckers' great-great granddaughter, who eventually married Walter Hauer's grandson and gave birth to triplets seven months later sparking rumors and gossip throughout the tight-knit kohlrabi growers community.

The decline of kohlrabi as a staple of households began in the 1920s largely due to the high taxes imposed by the Hoover administration. However, a recent surge in farms specializing in growing the original kohlrabi spiked after the discovery of a case of vintage kohlrabi wine found in Northern California in 1967. The wine was sold mainly in San Francisco during the summer of 1967, but spread slowly among locals after they reached their forties in the mid-eighties. Today the Confederation of Organic Kohlrabi Growers boasts a membership of six farms mainly located in area of Humboldt County, California.

Perhaps one day kohlrabi may rival its cousins cabbage, broccoli, cauliflower, kale, Brussels sprouts, collard greens and gai lan. Until then the black sheep, or should I say green sheep of the *Brassica oleracea* family shall remain unappreciated by connoisseurs of great vegetables of today.

The Critic

Condredge Baxter-Halloway III strolled regally into the Metropolitan Museum of Post Impressionist Art in Mayfair, South Dakota carrying an archaic brown leather briefcase. He proceeded directly to the gallery exhibiting the vast collection of Dutch painter Gillis van Dalem. He scanned thirty Warholianesque paintings before locating the piece his newspaper employer, *The New London Imperial Gazette*, had dispatched him on this long, tedious journey to review. He tilted his head as his sharply analytical mind scrutinized the previously unknown masterpiece. He gingerly set the briefcase on the faux marble floor, removed his deerstalker hat along with his tweed cape and deliberately placed them on the slatted, well-varnished wooden bench. He clenched his unlit Stanwell pipe in his teeth and allowed it to bob up and down. He paced to and fro as he studied the 24 by 36 inch discovery. He perused the effects of the changing light. He harrumphed numerous times. At last satisfied, he sat on the bench, withdrew his notebook, smoothed the top page, spread his fingers, licked the tip of his sharpened pencil and began.

As a product of the most prosperous nation in Europe, van Dalem has obviously been influenced by the trade, science, and art of the Netherlands as opposed to the more important and culturally acceptable artistic centers in the sophisticated south. The upheavals and large-scale mutations of populations of surrogate mediary, and the sharp, yet expected, break with the traditional monarchist and Catholic cultural customs, has motivated and, yea, even compelled van Dalem to reinvent art entirely. A task which, though successful overall, often overshadows the characteristics representative of the Golden Age in the general European period of Baroque painting. Regularly skewing the quotidian idealizations and prestige of hierarchical splendor typical of prevalent Baroque work, most of van Dalem's creations, including that which established his prominence and notoriety, reflects the traditions of detailed turmoil inherited from earlier Netherlandish works of art. A distinctive feature of the period is the proliferation of distinct genres associated with the mythical, allegorical, though hypocritical, efforts of his peers.

Although the birth of a neo-capitalistic society is often cited in relation to the precipitous proliferation of artistic production in the Netherlands, the bounteous wealth of the vulgarian aristocracy may explain van Dalem's obsession with conventions previously avoided, or prohibited in their entirety. It does not satisfactorily explain the communal concern of the theoretical obligations of morally unencumbered pretentious patrons. Taking all of this into consideration, I can unequivocally recommend this last van Dalem work as less of a step in self-indulgence than a renewal of the expertise demanded by the collective consciousness of competition in the market place.

Halloway III set his pencil on the bench and appraised his review. Totally satisfied with his effort, he closed his notebook and returned it to his briefcase. He clenched his pipe and reached for his hat and coat.

At that moment two men in white, paint-spattered clothing approached the van Dalem work.

"Looks dry to me."

The other removed the 36 by 24 sign proclaiming WET PAINT.

116

Summertime In Sunny Severnaya

Taras Arkady rubbed his permanently stained dirty hand through his matted heavy black beard. He lay on his back under a thick goose-down comforter. The smell of freshly brewed coffee reached his nostrils. He absentmindedly reached out and felt Marat, his Siberian husky, lying next to him. When the sizzle of frying salo reached his ears, he moved out from under the comforter and sat on the edge of the thin mattress on the wooden bed frame. Marat jumped down and trotted into the cooking area only ten feet away on the opposite wall of the windowless, one-room dwelling. Taras groaned as he stretched his arms over his head. He turned back and forth in a vain effort to loosen the stiff muscles of his back. His neck cracked audibly as he bent his head to the side. He slipped his insulated boots over his thick woolen socks. The bed frame groaned as he lifted his 250 pounds and stood to his full height of six and a half feet.

Daria Zakhar turned around and waved her iron spatula at Marat. "You will get your share, but only after we have eaten." Her breath hung in the air like a cloud of frozen dust.

Marat barked once, then sat on his haunches in strict obedience.

"This is the last of the coffee, Taras."

"That it has lasted this long is indeed a surprise," Taras said as he grabbed his Mickey Mouse mug from the wooden shelf above the coal-fired stove. He poured a cup of the thick brew. He swallowed half of it as he put an arm around his six foot tall blonde companion. "I suppose I will have to make a trip into Severnaya soon."

"It cannot be avoided much longer. We are down to our last bottle of Double Blow."

"We cannot run out of vodka! Coffee I can live without, but not my vodka." His laughter filled the room. "I will be back in a moment." He grabbed his gloves and fur-lined parka.

"I tried to make it to the coal shed yesterday, but it was still blocked." Daria held her hands over the stove in a futile attempt to

117

keep them warm. "I could see most of it though."

Taras opened the door and peered into the bright sunshine. He took ten steps into the wind. He looked around, then spat at a pesky weasel. His face registered surprise, so he spat again. He traced his footsteps back inside.

"Daria, I have good news." His face beamed.

"What is it, Taras?"

"It must be summer because my spittle did not freeze until it landed on the snow."

Casablanca

I paid my twenty-five cents to Mrs. Wilkens at the ticket booth and went inside to see the new Warner Brothers movie *Casablanca.* Adrenaline coursed through my veins because the movie purported to be about the war. Since we had just invaded North Africa a few weeks ago and my brother had been part of that invasion, I had more than just a casual interest in the film. Although I have to admit I had to look on my world atlas to find Casablanca.

I was familiar with two of the three main stars—Humphrey Bogart, Ingrid Bergman and Paul Heinreid. Bogart I knew because I had seen *The Maltese Falcon* just last year. I knew Bergman to be absolutely gorgeous, but as for Heinreid, I had never heard of him at all. Listed on the poster outside the theater as co-stars were Claude Rains, Conrad Veidt, Sidney Greenstreet, Peter Lorre and Dooley Wilson. I had some familiarity with the director, Michael Curtiz, because he also directed two of my favorite movies *Captain Blood* and *The Adventures of Robin Hood.* Since this was a war movie I had hoped to see a lot of action and battle scenes.

After the opening credits the movie starts with a picture of a spinning globe and the narrator describes a journey that refugees trying to escape the war must take to flee Europe. Many of them end up in Casablanca in French Morocco. The murder of German officers on a train leads to the frenzied round-up of all suspicious characters. One such character is shot as he flees. The camera pans along a group of refugees as a plane flies overhead giving us our first look at the sign above "Rick's Cafe Americain." The plane lands and we are introduced to two major characters Major Strasser, of the German army, and Captain Renaud, the prefect of police.

The scene switches to later that night and we are introduced to the busy cafe and eventually the first glimpse of Rick who is playing chess. Though we later see there is no one playing against him. Peter Lorre appears and we learn he is responsible for the murders and gives the "letters of transit" to Rick to hold for safekeeping. Back in the bar we listen to music and are introduced to Sidney Greenstreet's character, Signor Ferrari, who tries to steal his piano player and then tries to buy the cafe, but Rick refuses. After tossing his girlfriend out Rick sits and talks with Captain Renaud (Claude Rains). Back inside Captain Renaud informs Rick that Victor Lazlo, who appears to be an important opponent to the Germans, is coming to Casablanca.

Bogart's character appears to be neutral in all matters and never gives a straight answer to anyone. The Germans have a "dossier" on him and Major Strasser reads part of it to give us some background about Richard Blaine. Rick sits at a table and talks to Major Strasser and Captain Renaud. He gets up and leaves and the scene shifts to the first appearance of Ingrid Bergman and a man with her. Bergman, who plays Ilsa Lund is dressed in white and I have to admit, she looks fabulous. The man with her we learn is none other than Victor Lazlo, played by Paul Heinreid. I remained uncertain at this point about the relationship between Lazlo and Lund, but I learned later. They are taken to a table and Sam, the piano player, sees her and it appears they know each other—my guess anyway. After Victor Lazlo talks to Captain Renaud and Major Strasser, he meets with a shady character and they talk about the letters of transit. Bergman then asks for the piano player to come to her table and we learn that they do indeed know each other. They talk about "old times" and she requests a song. He refuses at first. But she convinces him to sing it. There is a great closeup of Bergman as it seems she is remembering something from her past. We then see Bogart walk into the large open bar and he hears the song. He purposefully strides over to Sam and reminds him that he had been instructed never to play that song again. He looks up and sees Bergman and immediately because of the change in the music, we know they have a history. We see tears in her eyes as she looks at Bogart. Rick and Ilsa talk about a time they had been together in Paris at the beginning of the war.

The next scene is of Rick drinking and smoking alone in his office in the now closed bar. Sam walks in and they talk. Bogart bangs his fist on the table and says, "Of all the gin joints in all the

120

towns in all the world, she walks into mine." It is now very apparent that there had been something more than just a casual acquaintance between Rick and Ilsa. Sam starts playing the piano and Rick tells him to play that song for him because he played it for her. It is "As Time Goes By" and the melody is heard throughout the rest of the movie. The camera closes in on an obviously upset Rick and the scene fades as the music swells and then we see the Arc De Triomphe in Paris. The music switches to the French national anthem "La Marseillaise" and we then see Rick and Ilsa in a car together with smiles on their faces. The top is down and their hair is blowing as they drive in Paris and then in the countryside. He puts an arm around her and she rests her head on his shoulder. It becomes obvious they are in love and I eventually figured out this was a "flashback." They are shown in different places in Paris and Bogart has a line I thought rather humorous. "Here's looking at you, kid." I think it is intended to show the difference in their ages. They are soon dancing in a nightclub, then seen in what could either be a hotel room or an apartment. Bergman is wearing what appears to be a satiny nightgown and they sit on the couch and kiss. She tells him the man in her life is dead.

The next scene is what I expected the entire movie to be about. We see soldiers, tanks, planes and now I assume the action will begin. However, the war scene is short and is just to lead us back into Pairs where Rick and Ilsa are at an outside cafe. They are given a newspaper and read about the invasion of France and the approach of the German troupes into Paris. We next see them in a bar with Sam, the piano player and once again Bogart uses the "looking at you, kid" line. They talk and it becomes apparent they really don't know much about each other. Bergman tells him to kiss her as if it were for the last time and the music lets you know that something bad is going to happen.

By now I had given up on this being a real war movie and had reconciled myself to the fact that it was just going to be a "love story." Both Rick and Ilsa need to leave Paris and plan to meet the next morning at the train station. It is pouring as Rick waits for Ilsa. Sam arrives and hands him a note from her. Rick holds it in his hands and the camera focuses in on the note as the rain begins to dissolve the ink. Ilsa tells Rick that she cannot ever see him again, but that she does love him. Rick and Sam board the train at the last second and as Rick stands in the doorway, looking upset and forlorn, he crumbles the note in his hand and tosses it away.

The flashback is over and the movie returns to Casablanca. Rick is still drinking and Ilsa walks into the bar. They talk and she tries to tell him a story, but he ends up chasing her away. The next day Victor Lazlo and Ilsa visit the police station where Major Strasser tries to convince Lazlo to give him the names of underground resistance leaders across Europe. Of course he refuses.

Rick visits Signor Ferrari at the Blue Parrot in order to allow the police to search his cafe for the letters of transit. As Rick is leaving Lazlo walks in. It appears Ferrari is the head of the black market and Lazlo needs his help to leave Casablanca. Rick sees Ilsa and apologizes about his behavior the night before. She ends up telling him that Victor Lazlo is her husband and had been even when they were in Paris. I must admit this took me by surprise because in Paris it appeared that Rick and Ilsa had been in love and most likely sleeping together—lucky man that Rick!

There is much talk about the missing letters of transit and although everyone seems to know Rick has them, no one is able to find them. While Rick is sitting at a table having a drink a young girl approaches him and asks for advice. She is newly married and she and her husband want to get to America. Rick doesn't seem interested in her troubles, but later arranges for her husband to win a large sum of money at the roulette table. It seems as though the heartless Rick is a "rank sentimentalist" according to Captain Renaud. Lazlo visits with Rick and wants to buy the letters, but Rick refuses to sell them. Back downstairs in the bar, the Germans are singing a song. The French start singing "La Marseillaise" after Lazlo asks the band to play it. The band leader looks at Rick who nods his head. Lazlo leads the song as Ilsa looks on in admiration. I just love the closeups of Ingrid Bergman. Major Strasser instructs Captain Renaud to close down the cafe because of the effect Lazlo has on the people. Renaud blows his whistle and chases everyone out. Rick asks him on what grounds and Renaud says, "I'm shocked, shocked to find that gambling is going on in here." Just then one of the employees hands Captain Renaud his winnings for the evening. There are humorous bits like this all throughout the movie. You have to be listening closely to catch them all.

Lazlo and Ilsa return to their hotel room and she wants to know what her husband and Rick talked about. He tells her that Rick refuses to sell the letters and that he should ask his wife why. Ilsa doesn't tell him about her time with Rick in Paris. One thing I noticed is that whenever the camera focuses in on a closeup of Bergman. it appears she has tears in her eyes. It might have just been a very effective trick of the lighting department to add realism to the shots. Lazlo leaves the room to go to a meeting of the "underground" and Ilsa leaves to see Rick. When he walks upstairs to his room over the cafe she is waiting for him. She brings up Paris and eventually pulls a gun on Rick. He tells her to go ahead and shoot him, but she can't. They embrace and she tells him that she still loves him. They kiss as "As Time Goes By" is played. She explains how and why she married Lazlo and that he had been captured, shot and apparently killed. They had kept their marriage a secret for her safety. She wishes she didn't love Rick so much and he uses the line "here's looking at you, kid" again. I got the impression that Lazlo had been more of a father figure to her and that she really loved Rick. The fact that she fell in love with Rick only after she learned that her husband had been killed keeps her character from becoming just another woman having an affair. Rick seems to know that Lazlo loves her and needs her to continue his work.

Lazlo is brought back to the cafe by Karl, one of the employees, while Ilsa and Rick are upstairs. Rick has Karl take Ilsa back to the hotel while he talks to Lazlo. Lazlo now knows that Rick and Ilsa had been, and still might be, in love with each other. He knows the circumstances and doesn't attach blame to either of them. The police come and arrest Lazlo. Rick makes a deal with Captain Renaud to let Lazlo go and he will be able to arrest him later with the letters of transit. Rick visits Ferrari at the Blue Parrot and sells the cafe to him with certain restrictions. Back at the cafe Renaud arrives. Ilsa comes rushing in and asks Rick why her husband thinks he is going with her. Ilsa is under the impression that she and Rick are leaving together. Rick asks her to trust him. Rick gives Lazlo the letters and Renaud comes out of the office to arrest him. It appears that Rick has double-crossed Lazlo. Renaud turns to face Rick and is surprised to see a gun pointed at him. Rick forces Renaud to call the airport, but he calls Major Strasser instead. The Major realizes what is going on and orders a squad of police to meet him at the airport. Rick, Renaud, Lazlo and Ilsa arrive at the airport. Renaud instructs the guard to load Lazlo's luggage on the plane. Ilsa doesn't understand why Rick instructs Renaud to put her name on one of the letters of transit. Rick explains to her that she needs to be with Lazlo or else she will regret it later. Lazlo comes over to talk to Rick and Ilsa and Rick lies about her feelings of love toward him. Lazlo accepts the explanation and the engines start on the plane. There are closeups of Rick, Ilsa and Lazlo as the tension mounts strongly aided by the music. Rick and Ilsa say goodbye and she and her husband walk away to board the plane as she cries. Strasser arrives and after pulling his gun is shot by Rick. The police arrive and are told by Captain Renaud to "round up the usual suspects." Renaud and Rick watch as the plane takes off with Lazlo and Ilsa aboard. They walk away into the mist and Rick says, "Louie, I think this is the beginning of a beautiful friendship." "La Marseillaise" plays as "The End" appears on the screen.

Okay, this turned out not to be a "war movie," as I hoped, but only a movie set during the war. It is basically the story of the love triangle between Rick, Ilsa and Lazlo. I did see it two more times after the first night, but just to catch all the subtle dialogue that moves too fast to catch in one trip to the movies. I found that I enjoyed the movie, but whether or not this movie will be remembered twenty years from now, I can't say. I guess we will just have to wait and see what happens as time goes by.

Don't Worry, Dear, It Was Only a Small Fire

I wrote this several years ago and included it in my collection of short stories entitled *Grandpa, Lions and Kitty Cats.* I wanted to share it again because it saves me from writing a new blog for whatever day it is published. Actually, someone suggested I add some of my older stories. Thank you, Phineas.

Last week my sisters and I spent some time visiting our mother. I brought a copy of my latest story and let everyone read it. They laughed, at the appropriate lines, I hope. My favorite sister Barb, as opposed to my favorite sister Bev, suggested I write about something that happened a long time ago in our first house. I promised to give it a shot.

After living in apartments for two years, Sheila and I purchased a small house in Crest Hill. For dinner one evening, we made tacos. Sheila was expecting our son Kevin. (Not for dinner, he wasn't born yet.) She would brown the hamburger and chop the veggies. My only responsibility was to heat the oil and cook the tortilla shells. I would heat the oil until it was rather hot, then dip the corn shells into the pan for a few seconds. Just long enough to get them good and greasy. I accomplished my job without any trouble and we ate dinner.

Thirty minutes later, I was hungry again. I guess that happened a lot in my younger days. We had some of the taco fixings left, so I turned on the stove to reheat the cooking oil. Can you guess by now what happened? I'll explain just in case you haven't. I got distracted. It happened so long ago that I can't remember exactly what diverted my attention, but I'll blame it on Sheila. She discombobulated me somehow and I forgot about the oil. (Another big word crossed off my list.) When I did remember, I ambled into the kitchen from our living room. I could tell immediately that something was amiss. My powers of observation were more acute in my twenties. I was almost positive we didn't usually have a fire shooting from the stove to the ceiling.

125

Within a few seconds, or a couple of minutes, I can't recall, my brain processed all the facts. Grease fires could not be extinguished with water. Right. Don't throw water on the fire. Got it. I thought of salt and grabbed the salt shaker from the table. I looked at the fire. The half-filled, or was it half-empty, salt shaker wouldn't be of any use, so I carefully placed it back on the table next to the pepper shaker. I can't remember if the pepper shaker was full or not. What else could I use? I scratched my head like Stan Laurel would do when Oliver Hardy would confound him. Then out of the corner of my eye, I spotted a blue coat. Aha! I can use this coat to smother the fire. Smart thinking, right? Not exactly. I grabbed the coat and covered the pan of burning oil. I can't remember if it was Wesson oil, or what brand. These days Sheila tries to use healthy cooking oils like coconut, or whatever else is the latest health-fad. Oh, yeah, the fire. I soon discovered nylon coats melt easily, but I did manage to smother the flames.

Good, the flames were out. I grabbed the handle of the pan, with the melting coat still on top, and raced out the back door while being careful not to spill any of the the oil on the faded, worn carpet. I paused to wave hi to my neighbors, then dumped everything in the grass. Luckily, the grass didn't catch on fire. I sauntered back inside and into the living room where Sheila sat on the couch reading a romance novel.

"Don't worry, dear, it was only a small fire, and I put it out already," I said as if small fires were as commonplace as taking out the garbage.

She smiled at me and said, "That's sweet." Then turned her attention back to her book.

I chose that moment to look at my hand. I suppose the brain takes a few minutes to process the info because I had suffered a second degree burn. It didn't hurt, yet.

"I think maybe you should take me to the hospital," I mentioned in a calm, matter-of-fact voice.

"Why? I just got to the good part," she replied. (I'm making that up just to add some hilarity to the situation.)

I waved my hand, which now hurt like... well... like a hand that had been burned. "The small fire, remember?"

She realized I was serious for perhaps the first time in my life. I think she drove to the hospital. Unless it sounds better to have her reading her romance novel while I drove. You can choose which version you like better and let me know.

We arrived at the ER and I walked up to the desk while Sheila continued to read.

"Can I help you?" the young volunteer asked as I noticed the same romance novel in her hand.

I thought, but didn't say, "Nah, I'm just browsing." I explained about my burned hand, and she told me to take a seat. I looked at the 268 other people waiting, including one skeleton, who I'm sure had been there a while. I turned back in time to hear an older nurse explain to the young volunteer, who was working her first shift in the ER, "We take burn victims in immediately."

By this time my hand hurt like... you know. The experienced nurse had me stick my hand in a pan of ice water. I thought about dumping it on my head, but didn't. They had to cut off my wedding band, which bothered Sheila for a second, but then she picked up her book again. I left the ER with my hand wrapped up in about five yards of gauze. I couldn't get my coat on over my hand. I obviously couldn't drive, so Sheila grudgingly set her book on the seat and drove me home. She pulled into the driveway, grabbed her book, hopped out and spotted a lump of melted blue nylon by the back door.

"Is that my new coat?" she asked as she frowned.

I nodded and said, "Maybe we should buy more salt the next time I go to the store."

Not That Choir... *The Choir*

I just returned home from an evening of choir music. I'm not talking about the Mormon Tabernacle Choir, but something much better. The Choir is a band based in Nashville, Tennessee. For those of you who have never heard of them, (shame on you for starters) The Choir has been together since the early 80s, releasing their first project in 1985. But enough of the background. Google them if you want to know more. Derri Daugherty and Steve Hindalong along with Dan Michaels, Tim Chandler and friends continue to make relevant music to this day.

Tonight's concert was an acoustic set in an intimate setting in Aurora at the Warehouse Church. There! I got a plug in for you Pastor Randy. I don't remember how old I might have been when I first saw these guys in concert, but I never get tired of seeing them perform. If you think bands have to be loud and obnoxious and an acoustic set sounds boring, you couldn't be more wrong. Great songs are great songs whether they're performed by a full band or two guys. Being a drummer myself, I pay close attention to other drummers. Steve Hindalong is not a drummer (like me). He is a professional percussionist. There is a world of difference. Derri Daugherty is the guitarist and lead singer. My cousin remarked he could instantly recognize Derri's voice whenever I played some of the older material. My cousin (he won't let me use his name in the blog, so let's call him... Andy) Anyway, Andy was a late comer to CCM. Now he loves The Choir.

After the show we talked to Derri and Steve. Can you imagine doing that at a Maroon 5 show? Not sure why I used them as an example, but I think they're playing at the Super Bowl this year. To me and their fans, these guys are Rock Gods. I couldn't begin to calculate how many hours I've listened to their music over the years, but if you get to know them like many of their fans have, you will realize they are kinda like normal people. Imagine that! They deal with the same things regular people do. In my books I have a character who is a famous rock star, but whose wife thinks he's a dork because he is so normal (boring). I'm not saying these guys are boring... they aren't. They are extremely talented musicians. And funny to boot. Don't take my word for it. Check out their website and buy some of their music. Amazon has everything. They also have solo projects, too. They keep getting better with each new project. Derri can even sing the older material in the same key as originally recorded.

Make a special effort to see The Choir when they come to your town. I guarantee you will not be disappointed. Andy guarantees it too.

An Entomologist's Work Is Just Bee-ginning

Have you ever noticed how young children go through phases? I'm thinking about how boys want to be firemen or policemen. Ben was no exception. However, near the end of the summer he became fascinated by bugs. All types of bugs, insects and other creepy, crawly things. He was elated whenever someone found a bug for him. A live praying mantis was the top of the mountain. I would have written 'cream of the crop' but I try not to use too many cliches. Anyway, I've been working on another chapter for the next book in the Emmy's Story series, and this came to mind. Though these books are complete fiction and bear only a slight resemblance to actual living people, some things in the stories have come true. Just sayin'.

"Kenny! Kenny! Where are you?" Emmy hollered as she raced down the hallway toward the family room.

Kenny dropped the TV remote, spit out the water he had been drinking and struggled to get up from his recliner. He succeeded and then stubbed a toe on the table. He quashed a mild expletive and yelled, "In the family room, Em. Are you all right?"

Emmy slid down the polished, hardwood floor in her white socks. She grabbed the wall and appeared in the wide, family room entrance holding up her phone. She saw Kenny hopping on one foot while trying to rub his toes. "Don't tell me. Did you run into the coffee table again?"

"You startled me. I thought maybe the house was on fire."

"The sprinkler system would come on, and you would be soaked." She suppressed a laugh.

"What's the emergency?" he asked. He plopped back into his recliner.

Heather, Isabella and Kevin rushed into the room.

"Mommy, we heard you yell," Heather said. "Did Miss Liz have the baby?"

Emmy nodded and pointed to the couch. "Let's sit down, and I will share all the details."

"I know she had a boy," Isabella said. "Natalie told me. She wanted a baby sister."

Kevin sat on the edge of the table holding a cardboard box.

"What's in that box?" Emmy asked pointing at it. "It better not be alive."

Kevin shook his head. "It's some of my bugs, but I think they're all dead now."

"It was easier when all you collected were firetrucks and police cars," Emmy said looking at Kenny.

"I might still be a fireman, but I want to be a bug scientist first," Kevin said.

"Kevin Michael, maybe you should leave your dead bugs outside."

"Tell us about the baby," Heather said as she squirmed on the couch.

Emmy checked her phone. "Okay, we all know it's a boy. His name is David Theodore. Tyler said that was his grandfather's name, but in reverse." Emmy motioned to indicate what she meant. "He is twenty-one inches long. He has some brown, fuzzy hair, and he weighed exactly eight pounds and two ounces. Poor Liz. He was a big one."

"Can we see the baby?" Heather asked.

"Maybe you should wait until they bring him home," Kenny said.

"But we're going on vacation on Saturday," Heather complained.

"Will Miss Liz come home before then?" Isabella asked.

Emmy looked at Kenny. "I'm not sure, but I want to see them. The girls are old enough to go with me."

Kenny shrugged and said, "If it's all right with Liz and Tyler, it's okay with me. Do you want to go, Kevin?"

Kevin looked inside his box and shook his head. "No, I have to find more bugs."

Emmy called Tyler a few minutes later.

"Liz says you can bring the girls. Dany was here, but she left ten minutes ago," he said.

"Are your in-laws there?" Emmy asked.

131

"No, they are in Hawaii. They won't be back for a week."

"We won't stay long, but I have to see the baby before we leave for Ireland."

Tyler chuckled and said, "Come on up. Room 4012."

"Who wants to go to the hospital?" Emmy asked.

Isabella squealed, "I do!"

Heather made a face. "Mom, you make it sound like we're going to Sainsbury's to go grocery shopping. We're going to see baby David. I hope they don't call him Theodore. That sounds like a name for an old person."

When Emmy and the girls arrived at room 4012, Tyler motioned for them to enter. "He's sleeping right now."

The girls approached slowly.

Liz smiled holding David in her arms. "You can look, but maybe you shouldn't hold him."

The twins moved close enough to see him.

"He's so tiny, but Mommy said he's big for a baby."

Isabella added, "He doesn't look all red and wrinkled."

"Emmy, do you tell them all babies look like that?"

Emmy bit her lip for a second. "I might have mentioned something along that line. I told them some babies have a funny-shaped head, too."

"He looks normal," Heather said.

"Did we have lumpy heads?" Isabella asked.

"I don't remember," Emmy said. "I was kinda out of it after you were born."

"I've heard some stories about that day," Liz said. She glanced at the twins. "It was an exciting day."

"That's for sure," Emmy said. She stood behind the girls and smiled at David. "He looks just like Tyler."

"Does he really, Mommy?" Isabella asked.

"No, but I like to say that to fathers."

"Since this pregnancy was easier than the others, I told Tyler I want two more babies," Liz said while grinning at Tyler.

Emmy looked at him, too. "What was his reaction? I bet I know."

Liz rolled her eyes. "He groaned and shook his head."

132

Behold The Terrors Within

Fortunately, I was able to retire at an early age while my wife still worked. Being the kind, considerate husband, I decided to take on some of the household chores. I could turn on a vacuum cleaner with ease. I could even run it over the carpet and hardwood floors and remove a modest amount of dust and other debris. Where does all that dust come from? If I didn't remove it, would the house eventually become filled floor-to-ceiling with dust? I could remove the contents of waste baskets without breaking a sweat. (Had to include a cliché, or two) I even tried my hand at preparing the evening repast. Within a week I had lost five pounds because of my inability to turn Hamburger Helper into a *nutritious* meal. When did they start putting nutrition labels on the side of boxes? And who, besides wives, ever reads them? I decided to let the professionals take over. I still did the grocery shopping and I even read the labels listing the ingredients, though I had no clue what most of them were. What is unbleached monosodium biphosphorous glutamtin? Definitely sounds like a natural ingredient to me.

One chore I took over immediately was the laundry. I thought it a rather simple and mundane task. In our closet are three plastic tubs. Color coded to simplify matters. The white basket is for whites. Duh! But then why are the multicolored towels tossed into that basket? The blue one for colors and the other one, which is stuck back in the corner almost out of sight, is filled with...I don't actually know, but I was instructed to never touch that basket. I suspect it contained... *unmentionables*. We had a new warshing machine (Misspelling intended because that's how I pronounce it much to the dismay of my wife) and a dryer. After I earned my PHD in advanced bio-mechanical electrical engineering with a masters in computational statistics and programming, I figured out which button to push to make the thing work. It was so much easier to pound clothes on rocks in the stream behind our house, but due to complaints from the government department of SWCITC (A prize to the first person who can tell me what that acronym means!) I continued to use the newfangled warshing machine. I miss my oldfangled rocks. I would happily do load after load of clothes as I sang Bohemian folk songs to Scout and Treat, who invariably scampered away to hide under the bed. The cowards! I used the dryer effectively. Do you know that those dryer sheet things will last for close to a month before they disintegrate?

However! There was one task I could not master. Folding clothes. No matter how hard I tried, I could not get my handkerchiefs to resemble a square. Octotrapezoids, yes. Piece of cake, but not squares. I negotiated for a week and after giving up golf and any hopes of ever owning a red Porsche 911, I turned that chore over to my wife. At least now I had square handkerchiefs and, even more importantly, wrinkle-free t-shirts. Even my briefs, boxers and the ones that can't quite decide if they are briefs or boxers, were folded neat as a pin.

Life was idyllic and the years passed. Grandchildren were born, grew up, went to college and... no wait, that's just in my daydream. The grandkids are still young, cute, adorable and still love their Gra. Facebook research proves that any mention of cute, adorable grandkids is worth 8.38 extra 'likes.' About ten days ago my wife approached me at the negotiating table (my comfy recliner) with a new offer.

"I'll let you start playing golf again and you can even buy a used 911..."

My ears perked up and a minute later, I opened my eyes.

"...If I don't have to fold your underwear anymore."

Already, the old t-shirts I wear to bed were haphazardly tossed into the nightstand on my side of the bed. Now I needed to make a decision. Could I get used to unfolded underwear? I consider myself open to new ideas. I actually own a cordless phone and a Xerox 6016 Memorywriter word processor. I dug out the old clubs, looked online at the price of used 911s. If I could only find a 1963...

"All right. You don't have to fold my briefs, boxers, or those other things."

She chuckled as I caved. I think she already knew my back

would not allow me to swing a club like Tiger Woods anymore. Oh, wait. He can't swing a club, either. What's the name of that new guy... How did my wife know I couldn't get in or out of a Porsche 911 without the paramedics standing by to insert and extricate me.

So, what did I gain by allowing her to spend more time sitting on the couch with her laptop instead of standing by the laundry counter (otherwise known as the dining room table) folding clothes? Nothing, really. What did I lose? I realized that the first time I opened the second drawer from the top and beheld the terror within.

Why Can't Car Keys and Electrical Outlets Be Friends?

"All burned up! All burned up!"

I heard these ominous words as the bathroom door opened suddenly. I had just stepped out of the shower. I wrapped the towel around me as I listened to my son shouting over and over as his little sister nodded her head in agreement. Being an adult of moderate intelligence, I immediately understood that this could be an indication that something was amiss. I followed the kids out of the bathroom and into the hallway.

My wife had gone back to work at AT&T since the kids were now old enough to do some things on their own—eat, drink, make a general mess of the house. They were both walking, and in the case of my son, running, on their own. Or maybe we just needed the money, I can't remember for sure. Anyway, I was babysitting the two monsters... I mean adorable siblings and...

"All burned up! " My son repeated as he pointed to my keys on the floor.

His sister pointed at the keys, too, or maybe she pointed at her brother. I can't remember for sure, but I assumed her to be innocent in the matter.

"I get that part," I said. "What happened?" Neither one made a sound. "Now you decide to be quiet, huh?" I looked at the lone outlet in the hallway and noticed some black streaks. I picked up my keys and noticed the same black smudge. I didn't need to call Sherlock Holmes to figure out this mystery.

Every cabinet door in the house had those irritating childproof fasteners that only impeded me from opening the doors. All the outlets had those plastic safety thingamajigs, I don't know the technical name for them, that prevent anyone over the age of five from sticking objects into the outlet.

"How did this...? Where is that stupid plastic thingamajig?" My two-tear-old daughter pointed again. I spotted the vacuum cleaner at the end of the hallway and slapped my forehead. I checked their fingers for any sign of a booboo. They were both good to go—other than one of them needed a new diaper. I picked them up, hugged them and gave them lots of kisses.

"Maybe we shouldn't tell your mother about this when she gets home." They both nodded in agreement.

Several hours later my wife walked in the back door. I was sitting on the couch in the living room holding two sleepy kids on my lap as I read one of their favorite books for the umpteenth time. As soon as they heard their mother call out, "I'm home!" they instantly re-energized. They scrambled down from my lap and ran to the kitchen.

I heard my son, the traitor, shouting, "All burned up!"

I knew I should have made them *pinky swear* never to tell.

Notre Dame Defeats Electoral College... Again

The University of Notre Dame's Fighting Irish football team soundly defeated the Electoral College Lyres yesterday afternoon in front of 83,000 fans in William Hillary Stadium. With a final score of 538-0, this marked the largest margin of victory in the series which began in 1842. The Irish scored on every possession and dominated the game from the opening kick-off. The Electoral College Lyres campaigned hard but were no match for the strength and size of the imposing Irish.

Notre Dame head coach, Millard Fillmore VI, not wanting to run up the score pulled his starters early in the first quarter and finished the game with players in mascot uniforms. After the game Coach Fillmore was quoted as saying he would have played his starters longer, but many of them needed to finish homework assignments. Starting Irish quarterback, George Gipper, was seen on the sideline assisting local school children with science projects.

Thomas Pinckney, long time coach for the Lyres, issued a statement after the game praising his team for holding fast to their obligation to provide entertainment for the enthusiastic crowd. He declared it was more important to win the popular vote of the fans than please the college alumni.

Though it was later determined by the cleanup crew that 21,042 of the 83,137 fans in attendance were actually deceased and should not have been counted in the attendance figures, Electoral College chief statistician, Hilda Napolitanoski, defended the count while pledging to monitor the situation more closely. When questioned about this the next morning, Pinckney dismissed the count insisting the people had been alive when they entered the stadium.

Electoral College President Jerry Bidden expressed concern after the 98th consecutive loss by his team. He hinted the college may drop football in favor of adding a croquet team.

In other news...

Archaeologists working in northeastern Turkey have uncovered the lost city of Soylecithin thought to have been the capital of ancient Pyrophosphateolis. Dr. Walton Henry Jones, the head of the Marshall College expedition, announced the discovery of facial coverings and Twinkies still in their original wrappers. The age of the site was determined to be from around 3174-3156 B.C. Dr. Jones was deciding whether or not he should sample the Twinkies which appeared to be in pristine condition.

Mom! The TV Repairman Is Here!

I remember the first television my parents ever purchased. It was in the mid-fifties and it appeared gigantic to a small child. I don't remember the brand name, but in those days a TV was a piece of furniture. The cabinet was more important than the screen.

We had two important pieces of furniture in the living room other than the couch and matching chair. One was the television and the other was the combination radio and record player. I remember the brand name of the radio because I went downstairs and checked. It was an RCA Victor and the label is still attached inside the door. That's right! I still have it in my basement. It hasn't worked for thirty or forty years... I'd be afraid to plug it in. It might blow up. But I still have it! For years I used it to hold my stereo components. Not inside the cabinet but stacked on top. This console served different purposes over the years. Its original purpose was to listen to Cardinal games on the radio. There was... and still is... an antenna coil in the back. It only received AM stations because FM wasn't a thing back then. Edwin Armstrong developed it back in the thirties, but it wasn't anything like we have today. But that's another blog.

Our radio/phonograph console had not one but two turntables in the cabinet. That's right! We had two record players. Pretty fancy for Kinmundy in the early fifties. One turntable played 45s and the bigger turntable in the bottom of the cabinet played 78s, 33s and 16s. What? You've never heard of records played at 16 and a third revolutions. They were used for spoken language and are rather rare today. The lone speaker was in the bottom right. Two turntables but only one speaker. Go figure.

My parents had a small collection of records. Mostly 78s and 45s. They favored Country & Western (That's what it was called back in those days) and Southern Gospel. I listened to Hank Williams, Hank Snow, Eddy Arnold, The Blackwood Brothers, The Statesmen Quartet and other similar artists. Somewhere in the house there might still be a few of the old 78s. I'm saving them for my old age along with my collection of ancient baseball cards.

When Mom decided to get rid of the old TV and radio consoles, I jumped at the chance to claim them. I used the old TV as a stand for my more modern TV, and you know how I used the radio cabinet.

Back to the television though. In the early fifties television sets used cathode ray tubes and other assorted vacuum tubes to produce the image and sound. Some sets might have up to 36 tubes inside. I didn't count them as a child, but saw that info on Wikipedia so it has to be correct. Right? Anyway, the tubes would not last forever. Right in the middle of an important television show, the set would go black or fuzzy or snowy. It just wouldn't work correctly. Dad would place a call to the TV Repairman, and he would show up at the front door almost instantly carrying a large case. He would set the case on the floor and open it. It was filled with vacuum tubes of all shapes sizes and other technical electric stuff . I would watch patiently as he risked life and limb to find the faulty tube and remove it. That's true because those tubes could hold a charge even after the TV was unplugged.

He would inspect the faulty tube and scratch his jaw. He would compare it to many in his case. Eventually, he would pull the correct the replacement out of his case of hundreds of tubes. We would have a picture again. At least until the next tube broke. The TV Repairman was a superhero to us kids. Not only could he replace the faulty tube, he could adjust the temperamental vertical and horizontal hold buttons so the image didn't flip up and down or from side to side. Modern TVs don't even have those controls anymore. Too bad.

Alas, there are no more TV Repairmen left in the world. No more cases full of magical vacuum tubes to be opened to the delight of children. TVs are disposable now. If it breaks, it is tossed away, or maybe recycled.

I still remember a time when you could call your local superhero and he would appear at your door to fix the fancy piece of furniture sitting in front of the picture window in your living room. Do I miss having an old unreliable TV? No way, but I do miss the TV Repairman. He was my friend. Thank you for all you did, Lew Hendricks. You are still missed and remembered.

Santa Claus Is Real... I Met Him In Person

I was talking to two of my grandkids the other day and the conversation turned to Christmas and more specifically the subject of Santa Claus. My grandkids are old enough now to question the concept of Santa delivering gifts on Christmas Eve. They see the Amazon trucks delivering packages all the time.

When one of them told me Santa wasn't real, I shook my head. I sat them down on the couch on either side of me and told them I knew a secret about Santa Claus, but they would have to promise not to tell anyone what I was about to divulge. They grinned and agreed to keep my secret. This is what I told them.

When I was younger, I actually didn't write books. I worked for a retail chain. They struggled with the concept of me as anything other than a grandpa. I told them Grandma even had photographs of us as younger people. They laughed but agreed to keep listening.

One day in early December I was working in one of our busy stores. Part of my job was to be friendly toward the customers. I would listen to their requests, complaints and suggestions. When I finally had a chance to walk around and check the store, I happened to see a man dressed rather plainly in brown pants, a red flannel shirt and black boots looking at the toys. I waited at the end of the aisle and watched as he inspected several of the most popular items. He laughed and shook his head. His large potbelly quivered like Jell-o. His wire-rimmed glasses were perched precariously on the end of his large nose. He ran a hand over his full, white beard and chuckled again. He noticed me watching and smiled. I approached him and asked if he needed any assistance. He replied he was only waiting for his wife to finish shopping.

I stared at him for a moment and since no one else was in the aisle, I asked if he lived in the area. He shook his head and pointed to the north. He was only visiting our town. I told him to have a pleasant holiday and was set to walk away, but something told me to stay. I watched him for another moment. He smiled and hummed a familiar tune. Maybe it was the child in me, or something else, but I told him he looked like Santa Claus. He guffawed and whispered he heard that a lot but mostly from children. I told him I had taken my kids to see *Santa Claus* at the local fire station, but they were not impressed by the man dressed in the red and white costume. He asked their ages and I answered. He asked if they had any special requests for Christmas. I mentioned a couple items from their lists, but mentioned I had not been able to find them in any store. He nodded and said something about those toys being rather scarce. I told him to have a happy holiday and walked away. As I turned the corner at the end of the aisle, I glanced back. I certainly didn't expect to see what I did. The man glanced around to make sure he was alone. He smiled at me, put a finger to his nose then whispered, "Ho! Ho! Ho!" I smiled and waved goodbye.

I didn't think about the man who resembled Santa Claus again until Christmas morning when the kids were opening their presents. When they both squealed with delight and hollered, "Where did you find this? This is exactly what I wanted."

I looked at my wife and she stared at me.

"Where did you find them?" We both asked simultaneously. Neither of us had found those toys in any store.

At that moment I remembered the man in my store and realized I had indeed met the real Santa Claus.

A Walk Into Town

"Hey, Paul, can we walk into town and get some pop?"

"Sure. You got any money?"

I smiled as I pulled out a wrinkled dollar bill and two shiny new quarters. "I got enough to last us all day."

You have now entered a time machine, and we're going back over sixty years. You will emerge from the time warp in the front yard of my uncle Charlie's farmhouse where Paul and I have been playing baseball for the last hour. It's summer with temperatures and humidity in the 90s. We are out in the country between Kinmundy and Alma. A half mile west along the Patoka Road is where Grandma and Grandpa live. That's where my mom grew up, and this is the scene of some of my favorite memories.

Paul tells his mom where we're going, and we walk down the gravel driveway to the tar and chip road that leads into the small town of Alma. Population around 450 and that might be stretching it. The road doesn't have a name, though years later when the 9-1-1 system is introduced, it will be named Malone Road. It's a narrow road with barely enough room for cars to pass. We walk a quarter mile south and enter the hilly section where it's not possible to see traffic coming over the hill until you reach the top. Fortunately, not many cars use this road. We are more likely to meet a tractor.

We amble lazily for thirty minutes or so, through shaded stretches of deep woods and open sections of farmland leaving footprints in the melting road, and finally reach the outskirts of town. We pass the grade school and make our way to the downtown area. For such a small town, Alma has several businesses pressed together in red brick buildings along the block-long street. Most of them on the north side which is where Paul and I are headed. We enter the first small grocery store - there are two in town at the time - and I immediately head to the front counter where the candy bars are stocked. I pick out six full-size bars and hand the cashier a quarter. Obviously, they were cheaper in the old days. We would share the candy as we headed down the street to another store where Paul would play pinball. After a few games, we would continue our leisurely stroll and end up at the gas station along Highway 37. Bottles of pop were kept cold in a metal cooler filled with ice. Our favorite was Orange Crush, and we would have enough money for a couple bottles apiece. I learned the hard way not to choose Grape Crush if the sun was beating down on us.

After spending an hour or so in town, we would begin the trek back to his house with money left over.

I remember another day when we decided to buy a frozen pizza. It was probably the first time I had ever eaten pizza. It's the first one I remember, at least. There were no pizzerias in the county to the best of my recollection. I don't remember why we chose a pizza, or how much it cost. Maybe Paul had eaten one before. I can't remember. I do remember by the time we got back to his house the once frozen pizza was a soggy mess. Aunt Mary probably thought we were crazy for buying something that needed to be cooked in the oven. Temperature and humidity in the 90s, remember.

I don't remember how that pizza tasted, but it must not have been too terrible because I still love a good pizza to this day.

At some point in time – the early 70s, I believe – Interstate 57 ruined our walk into town. Malone Road was split in two and detoured along the frontage road. We couldn't walk straight into Alma. Though to be fair, by this time we were old enough to drive. Driving a car into town to buy candy bars, pop and – well by now the store with the pinball machine had closed down and the pop and candy bars had skyrocketed in price. A dollar wouldn't last all day anymore. One Orange Crush and a Snickers bar would empty our pockets.

To this day I can't eat a Snickers or drink an Orange Crush without remembering the small grocery store in Alma and the walk into town. If someone invents a real time machine in my lifetime, I'm going back to that store, hand the cashier a quarter and stuff myself with six candy bars. Then I'll use my other quarter to drink enough Orange Crush to float a boat.

The Junior Class Carnival (and Other Important High School Activities)

One year my father was the junior class sponsor for the local high school. One of the fund-raisers for the junior class was the fall Carnival held in the old gym. That's the one in the picture. It was built in the early 20s if memory serves. Not that I was there when it was built, but... you get it, right?

I loved the old gym. It had atmosphere. It had an old-fashioned scoreboard with an actual clock to keep time. The new one was so different and modern. I think it was opened in 1957, maybe '58, but it was so big compared to the old gym. My dad coached the junior high basketball team in the late '50s. I think he might have coached some of the players from the '58-'59 team that went through the season undefeated. Those guys were heroes to me, and I wanted to play basketball for the Hornets when I grew up. Unfortunately, they lost to Centralia in the regional final. That was back in the days of the one-class basketball tournament and the small schools didn't have much of a chance against the large schools, but they did defeat Salem. I wonder how far that team would have advanced in today's tournament setup. Pre-COVID, that is.

I should thank Dolores Ford Mobley and Gladys Corrie See for maintaining the Kinmundy Historical Society site. I reference the school yearbook often along with the interesting photos of old Kinmundy.

I don't remember how many times I attended, or snuck into, the Carnival, but I remember one year more than others. I was a bit older now, and was allowed to stay longer. I loved the games and remember one in particular. There were balloons and you threw darts at them. My aim was particularly good that night, and I popped more balloons than anyone in the history of the Carnival. Maybe just a slight exaggeration there. If I won a prize, I don't remember it, but I was enjoying myself. I probably stuffed myself on candy and pop or whatever refreshments were available.

I know the older kids – high school students – were focused

146

on the dance and the Carnival Court. I doubt if I was allowed to stay for the dance or the crowning of the new King and Queen. For some inexplicable reason, the junior class candidates always seemed to win and would be crowned king and queen of the Carnival. A coincidence? I think not. The voting must have been rigged. Oh, well, I guess some things never change.

One thing about the school yearbooks has always puzzled me. Oh, my dad was the faculty yearbook (or annual, as they were called back in the day) sponsor for a few years, and I would get to attend the meetings occasionally. The meetings were held in one of the basement classrooms – the typing room perhaps? My memory is a little fuzzy – and I got to hang out with the big kids and run up and down the stairs. Anyway, I have always been astonished by how much older and mature seniors look in yearbooks of the '40s and '50s. Why is that? They were seventeen or eighteen-year-old kids just like the graduates of today. Was it just the fashions or hairstyles of the day? Was it due to the black and white photos? It's a mystery to me. Maybe someday the answer will be revealed, but for now I gotta go. They just opened the free throw shooting contest, and I'm going to win it. I'm going to make more free throws than Bud, Garry, David, Chuck, Quentin and my other heroes from the basketball team.

The Farm

I had the privilege of having grandparents who lived on *The Farm*. Not just a farm, but *The Farm*. I'll tell you why.

When you have access to *the farm*, you have the chance to dig up worms, cut a pole from a tree, add a line, bobber and hook and go fishing in Grandpa's pond. There you might catch catfish, bluegills, or even an occasional small turtle. And all for free! You can't imagine my shock when, after we moved to northern Illinois, I learned you needed to buy a license to go fishing. What a ripoff!

My grandparents immigrated from Europe and wound up in Chicago where they met, fell in love, got married, survived the *Eastland* disaster and eventually moved to southern Illinois. Grandpa wanted to become a farmer after his career with Western Electric. Grandma wasn't thrilled to leave her family and friends, but she moved with Grandpa. Good thing or else I wouldn't be writing this blog. Wow! I probably wouldn't even exist.

Grandpa bought a 120 acre farm with a small house on the property. He added to the house over the years – probably as more kids were born. He built the barn, corn crib, the machine shed and several other outbuildings to house chickens, turkeys and other farm animals. Some of those buildings can be seen in the photo at the top of the blog. I don't remember the exact date this photo was taken, but the farm had changed a lot by them. When I was a kid, there were fences and gates everywhere. The fences would get a fresh coat of white paint every year or so. The yard around the house was surrounded by a fence. The barnyard was fenced in. The chickens had a fenced in area to hang out in. I remember tossing corn around and trying to get out of their way before they pecked me. The large garden in back of the house was enclosed. Check my blog about *wiffle ball* if you want to know more about that.

Grandpa could build whatever he needed for the farm (buildings, I mean). If something broke, he could fix it in his state-of-the-art (for the time) machine shop. The machine shop also housed the tractors and other farm implements. It was always a thrill if we got to ride on the tractor with Grandpa.

Did I mention the blue racer snake in the machine shop loft? Apparently Grandma, Mom or one of her brothers, saw the snake one day, and Grandma warned us kids not to play in the loft for the rest of her life. She must have thought snakes lived forever. I would climb into the loft every chance I had and never once saw a snake. Not even a mouse or other critter for that matter.

Grandma loved her flowerbeds. She would spend time making sure the circular beds looked perfect. Not easy to do considering she had to cook and feed the family, do all the canning of fruits and veggies to get them through the winter, mend the clothes, work in the fields and all the other chores associated with life on the farm. We never went hungry if we stayed with Grandma. She was the world's greatest cook even though I once told her her chicken and rice soup needed more rice to make it go farther.

In addition to the flowers and shrubs around the yard, there were trees in all the corners and, I think I remember a gigantic tree that stretched to the sky, not far away from one of the wells. It was certainly much too tall to climb to the top. I doubt if we could even reach the lowest branch. My cousin Paul and I loved to climb trees. He could climb higher because he lived on a farm and had more practice. I lived in the big city – Kinmundy had a population of 900, so it qualified as a big city in my eyes. Grandma would get after us because she thought we might fall. We never did.

We would play in all the buildings. In addition to the machine shed loft, we would climb to the top of the corn crib and of course the barn loft. The barn loft later became our basketball court after Grandpa stopped raising animals. That was great. We no longer had to bale hay and load the loft with food for the cows.

One of the chores I dreaded was loading the barn loft with hay bales. When Paul and I got old enough, we helped. Everyone worked on the farm. This chore was always done on the hottest day of the year, and we had to wear flannel shirts. Otherwise, the hay or straw would cut our arms to shreds. There is a difference between hay and straw. Many city folks don't know the difference. My uncles and Grandpa would bale the hay, load it on a flatbed wagon and deliver it to the barn. We had no machinery to move the hay from the wagon to the loft. We used muscle power. My cousin Carl was six years older than Paul and me. He could toss one of the bales from the wagon up to the loft. I think he did that to impress the younger cousins. It took two of us younger cousins to lift the bales. We would try to tackle him, but he was so strong, he could easily fend us off.

Grandma and Grandpa were so proud of the farm they built. It took a lot of work, but I do believe they enjoyed it. They have been gone for many years, and the farm has changed. I checked it out on Google Earth, and nature is reclaiming the fields where Grandpa raised corn, wheat and beans. The orchards once kept so trimmed and harvested, have disappeared. The pond is barely there. Several of the outbuildings are long gone. The fences have been removed to make it easier to mow. I'm glad Grandpa and Grandma can't see it now.

One of these years, the old house will be gone along with the remaining buildings. It's not the fault of anyone. It's just what happens to neglected farms. At least for now, I still have my memories and can picture the farm the way it was when I used to climb the trees, fish in the pond, suck the juice out of the Concord grapes, roll marbles along the floor in front of the fireplace, pick up the phone even though I knew it wasn't their ring, feed the chickens, play ball in the barnyard...

Yesterday, I Sat On a Bee, and It Didn't Sting Me

I wrote this after my mother passed away, and my son read it at her memorial service. I am posting this as my first blog on the new website.

Yesterday, shortly before six in the evening, I sat in a chair in room 206 at the nursing home and watched as Mom took her final breath. Then she slipped quietly away. Her struggles, pains and fears vanished in an instant. Mom was gone. She was free.

Mom had always been there. As a child, she comforted me when I fell off a contraption in the backyard and ran screaming into the house with blood pouring from my head. Apparently, that happened to me quite often. Many times as a child, and as an adult, I would listen to the story of how I cut my wrist after falling on the sidewalk while running with a glass of water out at Grandma's house. They rushed me to the doctor and he stitched me up. The jagged diagonal scar is still there on my left wrist. I can see why they were so concerned. She was there in the utility room when Beverly decided to insert her arm into the electric wringer, burning her wrist and necessitating another trip to the doctor. Not sure why she did that, and I'm sure Barb and I did nothing to convince her that might be a good idea. She was there when I found a large snake in the backyard shed and got scared. She read to me as a child and told me stories about growing up on a farm. I wish I could remember more of them, but as my cousin Carl said, "We weren't all that interested back then in what our elders had to say. We needed to go outside and throw rocks at each other." Or sometimes it was Mason jars filled with dirt. I think that might have been me doing the throwing and Paul's forehead on the receiving end. I don't remember how many stitches that involved. She took me to church every Sunday, and every other time the church held a service. I remember sitting through two-week-long revival services. Mildred Bryant would preach while her husband Earl fell asleep in his chair behind her. Why did he get to take a nap when we had to listen? She saved the certificates I received for memorizing Bible verses at VBS at the Kinmundy Methodist Church. She saved report cards, elementary school photos – do my ears still look that funny - and even saved the Cardinals baseball programs I collected on trips to Busch Stadium with my father. Yeah! I have Stan Musial's autograph. She saved everything.

The earliest memory I have is walking up the stairs in the terrifying, unpainted black house in Kinmundy to retrieve an old-fashioned Bissell Sweeper. I don't remember walking back down the stairs, but we did. Mom was always there. In the summers she played catch with me just like she did so many years previously with her youngest brother Bill. She must have done all right because Uncle Bill played baseball professionally.

On Friday, I will sit in a pew at our church and listen to Pastor Tyler talk about Mom. I'm sure he will do a great job because, unfortunately, he has had more experience doing funerals than any other twenty-seven-year-old. He also knows how to listen for just the right words to say. At some point, my tears will flow because that's just how I'm wired. I still can't watch *E.T.* or *Marley and Me*. At other times, I will smile because I will be thinking about the words Ben said in church last Sunday morning. Ben listened patiently to other people share about what God had done in their life the past week. Ben raised his hand and Pastor Tyler chuckled, as he often does, walked over to Ben, held the microphone and listened as Ben said a few words. His childlike trust in God evident. I'm sure I will be remembering more stories about my childhood in the days, weeks, months, maybe even years to come, and I will remember how Mom was always there. She is still there. It's just harder to see her now. I have to look inward… to my heart. Perhaps one day, if God allows, I will sit down with grownup Ben and tell him the story of how he once said to the entire church, "Yesterday, I sat on a bee, and it didn't sting me."

Check out these other titles by the author. Visit the website:
kennethleemcgee.com

The Emmy's Story Series

1. We Were 'posed to Get Married
2. One Of The Guys
3. A New Friend
4. Did You Like the Ravioli Tonight?
5. Completely and Forever: A Wedding
6. It's Time To Go!
7. How Difficult Can It Be?
8. Forever... Isabella... Forever
9. The Forgettable Year
10. Turning Thirty
11. Hello, I'm James
12. Remember The Struggle
13. But God! I Write Songs
14. A Lifelong Dream
15. Gideon's Tree
16. New Priorities
17. Christmas Surprise
18. God Is In Control
19. Life Goes On

The Annie Mercer O'Dell Series

1. Roosevelt High
2. North Park College
3. Smoky Mountain Summer

The Rex Ford & Clay Horn Books

1. The Amazing Adventures Of Rex Ford & Clay Horn

The Stockton Woods Series

1. Sounds Like a Mournful Train Today
2. Sounds Like a Happy Train Today
3. Sounds Like a Cheerful Train Today

Stand Alone Books

1. Growing Up In Kinmundy Junction
2. Grandpa, Lions and Kitty Cats: A Collection Of Short Stories For Children Of All Ages
3. The True Stories of Ol' Melvin, Obadiah, Perkins MacGhee and Other Characters
4. Grandpa, Lions and More Kitty Cats: A Second Collection Of Short Stories For Children Of All Ages

www.ingramcontent.com/pod-product-compliance
Lightning Source LLC
Chambersburg PA
CBHW032205190626
46810CB00018B/1571